THE BOY WHO COULD SEE SECRETS

THE MAGIC PEOPLE - BOOK 1

ANDI CUMBO-FLOYD

1

$\mathcal{A}$ wind had been blowing all afternoon, and Jedidiah Wilson knew something might be coming up behind it.

Behind the barn, the pines at the edge of the field were swaying and bending; in the gold of dusk, they seemed harbingers. Jed wasn't sure of good or ill. He pretty much didn't care, just so long as something happened.

Homeover was one of those towns where so little happened that even small things—new haircuts or fender benders near the IGA grocery store—became the talk at the post office, where most folks still picked up their mail every day.

Jed had been born in Homeover. Well, technically, he had been born over the mountain at the hospital in Lexington twelve years ago, so the locals considered him a native. However, his parents, from way up north in DC, were still "not from around here." Jed wished he could be anywhere else and considered not from around *here*. Some days, he pondered plucking out his arm hairs one by one just to feel something.

But on that day, April 2, Jed tasted change on the wind like he could taste the bacon his mama burnt every Sunday morning. It tainted the air and left the inside of his nostrils feeling just a bit raw.

He'd had hints of that taste before. That time up in the woods by the water tower when he'd seen that shadow moving among the trees, he'd gone home to tell his dad he'd seen Bigfoot. Or once at school after the had buses left, he'd stayed back because he thought he'd seen someone under the bleachers. The air had tasted burnt then, too, but not like this. Today, the whole world tasted that way.

Jed had been riding his bike up and down the driveway for an hour or two, just trying to keep his body busy. He had to stave off his anxiety somehow, and moving was the best way he'd found. Some days, he built little villages out of twigs he gathered at the edge of the woods, but today, his body needed bigger swings of motion.

As he pedaled, he cursed himself again for leaving his bike out in the rain; it had rusted, and he couldn't lower the seat, so now his knees were basically up in his chin. Combine that with the way his arms and legs were far too long for his scrawny white body, and Jed knew he was a sight. Or he would have been if anyone, anyone at all, had lived close enough to see him.

On his last pass up to the road, the feeling hit him at the back of his throat. He stopped hard, slamming his feet to the gravel so fast that a dust cloud puffed up around him. It was there, just behind the barn, he knew it. Before he could think, he was pedaling hard as he stood up on his bike for the ride down the small hill toward the farmhouse and the barn beyond.

He was so distracted that the swells of bedrock caught him totally by surprise. Suddenly, he was flying past the redbud trees at the bottom of the lane as his bicycle tumbled behind him. His arms broke his fall, and he felt them snap. He heard it, too. The pain seared up his arms, all the way to the back of his tongue, and he had to bite his cheek to keep from crying out. But he couldn't afford to stop.

He carefully rolled to his right side and used his shoulders and knees to lever himself to standing. Then, he was off again, his arms crossed and cradled against his body as he sprinted toward the woods. It was there. He had to make it.

As Jed jogged past the barn, he heard his dad call out and caught a glimpse of him rolling out from under their ancient International Harvester tractor. Normally, he would have stopped and said hi to his dad. Jed loved talking with him, even though he knew that wasn't cool in any way. Today, he just kept running.

A few hundred feet farther, he burst into the shadow of the woods. There, he stopped so quickly that his momentum almost sent him face-first into the ground again.

There it was. He could see it: a shadow amongst the shadows. A darker form, with a not-quite shape, was watching him. Later, Jed couldn't tell why he thought this, but he knew it was a kid, and a curious one. Perhaps a little scared, but mostly curious.

Jed took a gentle step forward, and the not-quite-thing pulled back behind a tree before slipping a bit of itself out again like it was playing peekaboo.

They played this game for a while, and each step brought Jed closer until he thought he could almost touch it. But of course, he'd forgotten that his arms were killing him. When he stretched out his hand, the sharp bolt of pain forced a scream out of his mouth. The childlike-form took off, running deep into the woods.

Jed knew it was not wise to chase anything or anyone into the forest. Still, he couldn't help himself. He tucked his arms tight against his chest and went in.

Here's probably a good place as any to tell you who I am. My name's Mavis, and I was Jed's best friend—had been since he was two. I had curly red hair that reached my shoulders, and I was the kind of white that never tanned. Some people might guess I had Irish heritage, but as far as I knew, I didn't have any heritage at all.

Jed and I spent all our time together when he was little, playing with his stuffed animals and racing cars around the cities we built from his favorite books. I ate dinner right beside him most nights, sitting in the chair across from his mom and minding my manners so I wouldn't get sent away. Sometimes, when Jed's parents were tired or upset with him, I'd have to leave.

At night, when it was time for Jed to go to sleep, I'd curl up underneath his bed and wait for him to wake up. Most nights, he slept soundly and only woke up in the morning. Sometimes, he'd have these nightmares about big black monsters that moved without sound; and on those nights, I'd climb up next to him in bed and let him tell me all about it before he fell back to sleep.

This is, of course, one of the fundamental duties of an imaginary friend, after all. Comfort. And I was good at comfort.

However, I wasn't in the woods that day with Jed. I was on the farm, as I always was those days; Jed didn't need me as much anymore. Mostly, I just gave him a wave from time to time. He never ignored me, even when it might have embarrassed him to be seen waving to someone no one else could see, but we didn't talk as much as we used to either. Guess that's natural for a sixty-three-year-old woman and a twelve-year-old boy. We just didn't have that much in common then.

So, I only heard about Jed's adventure later. Still, I'm the only one you're going to hear it from, so it'll have to suit. People take the words of those gospel fellows as—well—gospel, and two of those men wasn't there either, so I figure my word is good.

Anyway, Jed was following that maybe-child-form-thingy into the woods, and that taste just kept getting stronger and stronger in the back of his throat. So strong, in fact, that he started to choke on it. Then, for a second, he hesitated and thought about going back, but he couldn't. He just had to keep going.

He walked a good way into the Lacy's woods and past that into the Thorne property. Ahead of him—not leading him exactly, but not trying too hard to shake him either—that shadow moved on. Jed knew these woods well, knew they curved all the way back around Klinger Mountain without meeting a road. Once again, he thought, "Bigfoot. If only this were Bigfoot."

See, Jed knew people wouldn't believe him if he ever told them he saw things. He knew that people liked to entertain the idea of mythical creatures because it's fun, but they don't take too well to people who claim to do the actual magic. "Look at what happened to the witches in Salem and the characters in *The Magicians*," he was always saying to his parents when they'd get into their well-worn debate about the supernatural. Jed's parents were more open-minded than most, but even they didn't really think supernatural stuff was there, just that it could potentially be. Hence, Bigfoot. That was such a common and easily-dismissed myth that it was okay to hunt Bigfoot, just not okay to believe you might find him.

Jed knew though. He'd been seeing things since he'd been born. The ghost of that mine foreman over at that collapsed entrance. The way Susan Beth in town could say a few words to someone and heal up their flu or their knife cut just like that. The dark halo that followed Reverend Smithe everywhere. Jed literally saw what most people only sensed, and he'd learned long ago to not tell that to anyone—anyone but me, that is.

That day, Jed was seeing something new to him, but unlike most people, Jed wasn't scared by new. The things that he saw didn't frighten him at all. What did scare him—what made it so he couldn't ever quite sit still—was what these things meant about the people around him. When one of these things was linked to someone, well, it wasn't good. It wasn't good at all.

Maybe that's why he wasn't scared in the woods: no people, no problems. So, he kept on walking, that taste growing. The tiny hairs on the back of the neck that usually make people slow down stood up straight as new rebar.

He wasn't ready though, not ready at all. Maybe no one can be ready for what was to come. That lady in *Outlander* certainly wasn't. But one minute, Jed was in the woods he knew, skirting a big pin oak. And the next, he was in the same woods, but he didn't know them anymore. They were thicker, noisier with birds and critters. Ahead of him, he could hear singing. A woman singing, but not in any language he knew.

The shadow he'd been following had slipped farther ahead, and Jed didn't know what else to do but to keep going. So he walked on, arms folded against himself, stepping carefully so he wouldn't fall.

He walked right into a cluster of low buildings. It reminded him of the summer camp his parents had sent him to when he was eight. A cluster of small cabins stood around a big fire circle in the middle. All around, people were moving as they would in any village: running errands, making meals, and talking to one another as they leaned upon doorways.

Slowly, though, all movement and conversation stopped, and every eye turned to Jed, the only white man amidst a whole community of black people. Black people who looked very unhappy to see him.

2

*J*edidiah froze and thought, just for a minute, about stepping back and out of whatever place he'd entered. As hands slipped to knives and men rose from their card game, he decided he should stand stock-still.

He must have stood there for a while because he felt his arms really begin to ache, the kind of ache that feels like it'll break you down to tears if you don't focus only on it. He began to shake, and a cold sweat broke out on his head—from fear but also from pain—and he thought he might pass out when he heard a loud, clear voice.

"Leave that boy alone. Can't you see he hurting? Come here, child."

Jed looked to his left and saw a large woman with a gray scarf over her hair, waving him over from the doorway of a cabin. He stumbled her way, and she caught him by the waist, avoiding his arms carefully. "Boy, you done broke those arms o' yours. Sit." She pointed at a wooden chair in the corner of what Jed could now see was a cabin made out of scraps of lumber. Slivers of light shown through, and Jed could feel the cool of the early spring evening seeping into the room.

He collapsed into the chair and grunted as the impact jarred his arms. The impulse to lean his head against the wall behind him and let go of all the tears was fierce, but Jed fought back, sure he was there for a reason, and sure he needed to know that reason.

The woman pulled a stool in front of him and gently laid each of his arms against her own. Jed felt mighty awkward with that much physical contact with a woman he'd just met, but he wasn't in much of a position to argue. So he let her do her thing.

She began to sing, and Jed realized it had been her voice he'd heard through the woods. He didn't know what she was saying, but the tone was soft and sweet, like a lullaby. His arms began to tingle like they'd been frozen and were thawing out in warm water.

ONYE TIRI NWA NA EBE AKWA?

Egbe tiri nwa na ebe akwa.

Weta uziza weta ose,

weta amara ngiringa ofe.

Ka umu nnunnu racha ya,

ka okpodudu kpogbuo ya.

Egbe ndo, egbe ndo.

THE NEXT THING JED KNEW, he was in a warm bed with a light blanket over him, and he felt amazing. He started to sit up but stopped quickly, bracing for the flash of pain to pass through his arms. Nothing.

Gingerly, he stretched his forearms in front of him and flexed his fingers. Then, he bent his elbows, and when that still didn't hurt, he pressed one hand against the other. Pain-free. Completely.

He sat up quickly then and looked around the room. The woman was sitting just outside the door, shelling peas, and Jed thought of his grandmother on her porch doing the same thing on cool spring days. The thought made him wistful, but he didn't have time for nostalgia.

He got up, put on his shoes, which were tucked neatly next to the mattress, and went to sit by the woman by the door.

"Thank you," Jed said. A million questions were flooding his mind, but he knew his first bit of work was gratitude.

"Welcome, child. Those were some nasty snaps in those arms. You fell hard?"

"I did. Bicycle acci—" This woman wouldn't know what a bicycle was because bicycles hadn't been invented yet. "Yeah, I fell hard."

"Those two-wheeled machines can be dangerous. Best watch yourself."

Jed leaned back and tucked his chin against his chest. "You know what a bicycle is?"

"Course I do, child. I been where you live. Lived there myself until this wood brought me back." She dropped her last handful of peas into the basket at her feet, wiped her hands on her skirt, and looked at him. "Go ahead. Ask me what you want to know."

"Time travel. That's what I did, right?"

"Sure enough. You walked through a portal in time back there where that big pin oak is."

Jed looked over at the tree and squinted. "But I followed

someone here."

"Yep." She pointed to a little girl playing with a doll by the fire in the middle of the village. "Lizzie time walks too. Better at it than you are. Most people don't see her."

Jed almost took offense, even though he wasn't sure to what, when he saw the twist of a smile at the corner of her mouth. "I'm Jed. Jedidiah Wilson."

"Sharon Conover. Nice to meet you, Jed." She took his outstretched hand in her own. "Those arms feeling all right now?"

Surprised, Jed looked down at his arms and realized, once again, that they didn't hurt at all. "Yes, ma'am. You did that, didn't you?"

She stood up and picked up the pea basket. "One of many things we can do, Jed. One of many things. You'll see." She walked over to the fire and dropped the peas into the kettle hanging over it.

Jed had thought he'd had questions before, but now, he couldn't even begin to find words to fit any idea of what he wanted to know.

Just then, Lizzie came over, head dipped low, but eyes upturned. Her two braids hung against the pink plaid of her dress. "You saw me? No one ever saw me before."

He pondered a minute. "Well, I couldn't rightly see you. More of your shadow, or as if you were a shadow. I just knew you were there, and I knew I needed to follow you."

She smiled, her head still down. "You're one of us, then?"

"Us?" Jed shook his head.

"One of us." Lizzie waved her hand around the village. "One of the magic people."

She ran off toward a group of kids kicking a ball around. As Jed watched them, he realized they were kicking a very familiar ball —a black-and-white soccer ball like the ones the team used at school. Of all the things Jed had seen that afternoon, that ball was the most jarring. Somehow, it hadn't bothered him that he had traveled through time or that Lizzie had, too, but that ball. . . The fact that a ball could pass through centuries? That was too much. He thought he might throw up.

Before he could turn to go behind the building, a large man stepped up to him, laid a hand on his shoulder, and said in a very soft voice, "It's a lot. Was for all of us. Let's eat."

Jed looked up into the man's face and saw only kindness, so he followed the man to the fire and took a seat on a log beside it. Someone handed him a bowl that looked very much like one from a set his Aunt Minnie had, and he took a bite of the best vegetable soup he'd ever eaten. That first bite triggered his hunger, and before he knew it, he'd eaten the whole bowl and was hoping there was more.

Another man, slight and long-legged, took his bowl and filled it again without a word, and Jed smiled a *thank you*. People circled the fire, each perched on a log and eating silently.

Well, mostly silently. No one was talking, that was for sure, but Jed could feel a form of communication—like everyone there, including him, was tied together by some invisible thread. He imagined that game he and his real friends had played as kids, with cups tied to a string so they could talk over long distances. The words weren't clear, but there was a hum.

The longer he sat, the stronger the hum grew until he could almost feel it moving through his skeleton. No one was talking, but they were saying everything—not together, not some sort of collective, but a community bound together beyond words.

Jed had never felt more at home in his life.

JEDIDIAH

Mavis does a great job of speaking for me. She's been doing it since I was a tot. Just a little guy.

When I was scared or didn't want to do something, Mavis would say, "I know you're scared, Jed. I'd be scared if I was little like you too. Heck, I'm even a little scared now. But we all have to do scary things from time to time. You can do it."

Then, I'd look at my mom and say, "I'm scared, but I can do it," before I let go of her hand and jumped into the deep end. Mavis would already be there in the water; she was at the end of the lane when I rode my bike without training wheels for the first time, waiting for me. She was always there.

But this time, I needed to make sure I was heard on my own. I was terrified. Terrified when I saw that shadow. Terrified when I walked into that village. Terrified when Sharon healed my arms. If I could have climbed back into my own bed and started that day over again, I would have. All of that scared the bejeezus out of me.

So when Mavis said I'd never felt more at home, she was telling the truth, but only the heads-up side of it. The tails side was that I was so scared I wanted to pee my britches.

See, the part I hadn't told Mavis—until right this moment—was this: I could see the bad things coming already. I could feel them—like you can feel when someone's staring at you with malice in their hearts. I knew something was lingering out in the woods back there in the village time. Something that all them other magic people knew about, too, but Mavis. . . Mavis couldn't see it. And I needed her to be brave. For both of us.

_J_ed woke with a start when someone grabbed his ankle and nearly shook him out of the bed. It took him a minute to remember that he'd stayed the night in the village and a moment longer to remember the name of the man standing over him. "Alonso? What's going on?"

Jed had learned everyone's names the night before, around the fire. It wasn't a matter of introductions with words like his teachers always had them do on the first day of class: "Tell us your name, where you're from, and one fact that is unusual about you." Jed always hated that second question because he always had to say he was from Homeover. There was nothing exciting about that. And he always lied for the last one because, well, he wasn't about to tell people he could see the way history hung on people and places like shadows. He always lied and said, "I like brussels sprouts," and relished the wrinkled noses of his classmates.

But no, the night before wasn't introductions or even telepathy, at least not the way he thought about it. All words beamed from one person to another. It was more like he imagined the way he'd come to know his parents. There had been a time they hadn't known him, but he had always known them, known they were crucial, fundamental to who he was. The introductions had felt like that. . . Like he was becoming aware of people he had always known.

The fire had been dying down before the hum of connection had faded into the background like the sound of a running refrigerator. Jed had found himself ready for a deep sleep, not because of exhaustion but because he was so relaxed, all the way to the muscles against his bones.

But now, Alonso was jarring him awake in a way that only meant trouble.

"You have to go, Jed."

"Why, is something wrong?

"No. Well, not exactly. It's just that you can't be here when he arrives."

"He? He who?" Jed was bending down and picking up his pants from where he had dropped them in Alonso's cabin the night before.

"We'll have to explain all that later. But for now, you need to go back around the oak. Now."

Jed heard the urgency in the high pitch of Alonso's voice and jumped out of bed, shrugging on his sweatshirt as he went. As he sprinted toward the tree—he could feel it, the need to be gone —he waved to Lizzie.

She said, "See you soon."

Then, Jed skirted around the tree, and just like that, the forest shifted. More light poured in, and the animal noises quieted. He could still hear, very faintly, the songs of conversation from the magic people's village. Even louder, he could hear his parents calling to him.

He jogged out of the woods and up to the barn, expecting to have to make up some story about how he had fallen asleep, hunting morels or something. As he approached the barn, he saw his dad was still in the same clothes he'd been wearing the day before. He stood at the sink behind his shop and washed his hand with that red lava soap that really removed grease.

"Dinner's ready," his dad said over his shoulder. Then, he switched off the water and turned around. "You okay? You looked sort of, well, weird when you ran into the woods a few minutes ago."

Jed had read that wardrobe book, and his English teacher had made them read *Kindred* last year, so he knew that time traveled differently in different spaces. He couldn't shake the fact that he'd been gone for at least fourteen hours, and yet it seemed like only a few minutes had passed here.

He didn't have time to ponder it, though, because his mom, Anna, called them in for supper from the front porch of the farm-house. Jed took a detour through the barn and found me playing with one of the barn cats by the side door. "I have so much to tell you, Mavis," he whispered as he passed by. "Meet me in the walnut grove in an hour."

And that's how I came to know what had happened. I didn't quite believe him at first. It just didn't make sense that Jed would find a time portal thing in the woods where he'd lived his whole life. The more Jed told me about the people there, about the things they could do—healing, speaking languages without ever studying them, passing through solid objects, and growing plants where nothing else would grow—and the more he talked about the way he'd learned about these people and their talents through no words, the more my memory (or that thing that feels like memory, but is maybe just intuition) got tickled.

"These are spirit people, Jed."

"Spirit people? Lizzie said they're magic people. Are you saying they're ghosts?"

I shook my head. "Not at all. I'll have to spend some time remembering the details, but I just know about them: people who move not only in space, but also in time." I wasn't sure how I knew that, but I knew it for sure.

Jed was studying his hands. "It felt nice there, Mavis. Safe. Like I could be my whole self. But then, when they said I had to leave, well, I realized it was just like any other place where I didn't quite fit."

"It sounds to me like they were mighty hospitable to you."

"They were. Very. But they chased me out of there so fast."

"I expect that'll come clear soon enough." I had a sense of things, a sense that it would all work out. In this case, I figured nothing this big happened without some follow-up.

Sure enough, the next day, a long blue Lincoln Town Car, old but immaculate, pulled down the farm lane. Out stepped a tall regal black woman. She had a gray scarf wrapped around her hair. The moment I saw her, I knew it was Sharon.

Jed came out of the house with a dishtowel in his hands from where he'd been drying the lunch dishes, and I thought he might say something stupid with his mama and daddy right there.

"Jed, remember, they don't know." I pointed at his parents, and he gave me a slight nod without looking my way. We were old hats at flying under the radar now.

"How do you do, ma'am? What can I do you for?" Leon, Jed's dad, asked.

"My name is Sharon, Mr. Wilson, and I'm from the community center up on the corner." That center made the best breakfast every first Saturday of the month, and they used the proceeds to give scholarships to community high school students. "We heard that Jed here was really good at building things with unusual materials,"—those twig buildings were paying off—"and we wanted to see if he might be able to design and build a pavilion for us."

I gave Sharon a squinty stare, and she looked at me—right at me —and smiled.

Normally, Jed's parents would ask a million questions about how and why and when, and I was hoping that would happen here. I wasn't sure I was ready to let him go.

But I could tell by the way they were looking at Sharon that they hadn't even had to think twice. The moment she had opened her mouth, they were thinking, "Yes."

"If it's all right with you, I'll take him on with me now. Bring him back around dark."

"Sounds great," Anna said. "Jed, you have everything you need?"

I could tell from the look on Jed's face that he had no idea what he needed besides answers, so he nodded and walked to the passenger side door of the Town Car.

He gave me a wave as the car swung around the magnolia.

"That woman, Mavis I think her name is, she been your friend a long time, huh?" Sharon said as they pulled out onto the road.

"You can see her?"

"Like you, I can see a lot of things most folks can't. She's good people."

"The best," Jed said.

Jed told me all this much later, after all the adventure died down, but I never forgot it. You don't forget the first time someone else can see you.

At the community center, Sharon had set up a long stretch of paper and lots of pens and pencils. So when Jed walked in, he began to wonder if he really was going to be designing a pavilion.

"Your gift, Jed, is the gift of sight. Stronger sight than any of us have ever seen. We need you to draw for us the things you've seen. Show us what you've been shown."

Jed wrinkled his brow. He wasn't sure that he liked that this woman knew this much about him. It wasn't always easy to be the one who could see people's secrets, and despite Sharon's kindness the day before, he wasn't sure he could trust them. "What do you mean? I don't know how to draw."

"Yes, you do. You just haven't tried. Do it now." Her words weren't harsh, but they carried force.

Despite his reservations, Jed sat down at the edge of the long white table, started to grab a regular yellow pencil, but then decided on an old gray pen with a long tip and a well of ink. He placed his right hand on the paper, and then he started to sketch the shadow that hunted Rev. Smithe.

At first, he did those light strokes that we all use when we're trying to get a sense of the shape of a thing, but within a few minutes, he was pressing down solid and dipping that pen in the ink every few moments. Beneath his fingers, Reverend Smithe's long, lean face and dark hair, parted down the middle, began to form. There was the five o'clock shadow that was always there by noon. The slight hunch to his shoulders.

Then, Jed drew the thing behind the pastor—though, it was really around him—a fume almost. It clouded around the reverend and moved on its own, following him. On the page, the reverend's form and the shadow's shape were bound together but entirely separate, like Jed was drawing in three dimensions. He finished that sketch and kept going.

Once Jed started, he couldn't stop. He drew for hours. Lizzie's not-shadow in the forest. The girl under the bleachers at school. The glow that crossed Susan Beth's face when she spoke words to heal. The ache of loss that hung over the Gettysburg Battlefield, all dark but tethered. The glimpse of a lynched woman's feet he'd once seen at a canal lock outside Lexington. All of it.

By the time he was done, Jed had filled a football field's length of paper with images, and the room was full of people Jed had met in the village. Just about everyone come in and was watching, and Jed hadn't even noticed them arrive.

He slumped back against the folding chair and whispered, "I didn't know."

Sharon sat down beside him. "Most of us didn't know about you either, Jed. That's why we came. We needed to show you, but also to see."

"And we owed you an explanation," Alonso said. Jed saw Sharon cut Alonso a hard look, but the large man, who had seemed so intimidating to Jed at first, kept on talking as he pulled out a chair across the table and sat down.

"This morning, the man who considers himself our leader stopped by. David Poke is his name. He's a mean man, a man who thinks to control us."

"A man of his time," a woman's voice said from across the room.

"Yes, he's from the 1820s, and he's white, so. . ."

It took Jed a minute, history never being his strong suit, but he eventually got it. "He owned—er—owns slaves?"

"Right, and while he don't actually own us," Sharon said, "He think he do."

Alonso started to say more, but Sharon hissed at him, so he stopped talking and looked away from Jed.

Jed felt a shiver run down his spine. "That's awful, but what did that have to do with me being with you this morning?"

Sharon tilted her head and glared at him, and Jed realized the problem. "He might think I was trying to steal you from him."

"No one can steal us, Jed," Alonso said. "We come and go as we please, but white people—most white people—think what they want is most important. We knew right away you weren't like that, not from the way you came in all broken and still didn't ask for anything. But Poke doesn't know that you are aiming to take us. So it's best if you steer clear of him."

"Got it." Jed stretched his arms high above his head. "So, I'll just stay here and not come back to your village, especially since you all can come here." Jed paused. " Can he come here?

"He can't, but it's not that simple, Jed," Alonso said.

"Now that you've traveled, Jed, you've come into your power." A woman with long braids and a flowing purple skirt stepped out of the crowd. "Now, you have responsibilities. We don't have much time. I'm LaKeemba."

Instantly, Jed felt safe, protected. Something about the way LaKeemba held her presence in a room settled him. It looked like it did the same for everybody else too.

Jed stood and put out his hand to shake LaKeemba's, but she wrapped an arm around his shoulders. "Let's go get Mavis, shall we?"

4

To say I was surprised when LaKeemba walked right up to me, put out her hand, and shook mine would be an elephant-sized understatement. No one, not one single person in the entire world, had ever spoken to me besides Jed until that moment. I was speechless.

Then, LaKeemba said we had to go, and I stopped cold. "Go? I can't go nowhere. I'm bound right here—always have been, always will be."

LaKeemba looked back at a tall man standing behind her. He nodded, walked to me, shook my hand, and then walked a full circle around my body before he said, "Jump. Jump high."

I was so surprised, that I actually did it. I hefted my sixty-three-year-old girth into the air, and as I did, that man swept a leg under my feet. I felt a little tug as his foot passed under mine, and then, it was done. It was the oddest thing I'd ever experienced, and when you're mostly invisible, you have a lot of weird experiences.

"All right, then. Now we go." LaKeemba started to walk toward the woods behind the barn.

I gave Jed a look that said, *"She doesn't get it,"* and followed after her. I was sure I would not be able to go any farther than the old tree, which stood about ten feet from where the shadows began to gather in the forest.

But sure enough, as we passed that tree, I just kept on walking. I saw LaKeemba shoot me a sly smile over her shoulder as she headed into the tree line, and I whispered, "I'll be a monkey's uncle," as I followed her right in.

Jed walked right beside me, and sometimes, his arm brushed against mine. Poor kid was scared and confused, and I gave his forearm a quick squeeze as we walked. "This the way you went last night?"

He nodded. "Pretty much. See that big pin oak up there?"

"That's the one, eh? All right, I'm ready."

But there wasn't really anything for me to be ready for. I guess when you're not corporeal, so to speak, time travel is pretty unnoticeable. Of course, Jed was as bodied as a person could get, and he hadn't been bothered by the shift either. So, maybe all those books that make time travel seem like it flips your insides over were just full of it.

I didn't feel it, but I saw it right off. The clothes on most of the folks were what I'd call "old-timey"—that's the technical term. And no one in their right mind cooked over an open fire in the present unless they're trying to teach some young people a lesson about "roughing it."

However, the fact that we'd traveled through time wasn't really what I noticed. What struck me was that every person in that town was staring at me. Not just starting towards me. Not around me because Jed pointed to where I was sitting, but at me, at my face. It was creepy.

Jed, though, had trotted over to a man with shoulders as broad as a barn and was bringing him back my way. "Mavis, this is Alonso. He's a friend."

The man was looking me right in the eye, and the sensation was both nerve-wracking and so very profound that I felt tears gather by my tonsils. I was so used to only seeing Jed's green eyes peering into mine, but here—here was another person looking at me like I was a human, not just some idea that needed to be patronized to keep a kid happy.

"Nice to meet you, Mavis. I hear you're Jed's friend. It's good to see you."

I took his offered hand and shook it hard. "It's good to be seen, Alonso. Thank you."

"I know it is, ma'am. Spent a few years as an imaginary friend of sorts myself. It gets wearisome to always be hinted at but never addressed. I assure you that here you are every bit as real as any of us."

I'm not a teary person, but those words, they tipped me over the edge, and I felt a trail of water on my cheek. "Thank you. I'm glad you guys can all see me. That's a gift."

"Oh, it's more than that," Sharon said as she came up behind me. "Now, you'll be seen by everyone. Come here to Heavenland, and that makes you almost all of who you were built to be. And you, Mavis," Sharon put a heavy hand on my shoulder, "you was never meant to be imaginary. That's just a broken world thing. No, woman, you is as real as ever now. Welcome to the world."

About a million things were flying through my head, including how I'd find a place to live and whether or not Jed and I would still be friends, but I didn't have time to ask or even really think, because just then a loud bell rang from by the fire. LaKeemba, Sharon, and another woman had taken seats on a big log, facing out from the flames behind them.

"We can ask questions later, I bet," Jed said as we walked over to the fire.

He and I took seats in the grass in front of the three women. Jed dropped to the ground like he was made of string. I eased myself down slowly, trying not to groan out loud. You'd have thought that becoming real would have had the perk of knees that didn't ache, but no.

The rest of the folks in the village sat down with us, and we all waited. LaKeemba stood by the fire and held the silence for a while, and I felt antsy. The air was heavy like it was carrying something, and I was eager to see the load put down. I took Jed's hand and waited.

Finally, LaKeemba said, "Friends, you know we are under threat. Not just from Poke. We've all felt it—that shift in the air, the way our abilities come to us a bit slower, leave us a bit more tired. Something is coming, and that something isn't good for us."

I heard the murmur pass through the crowd in affirmation. Oh crap, this was about to get very real.

"So, we have two choices. We can wait and see what happens. Or we can prepare as we wait."

The rustle of fabric grew louder, and LaKeemba raised a hand. "I know. You ponder how we can prepare when we don't know what's coming." She turned to the woman on her left. "Shelby has had a vision."

Where I'm from, everyone would have murmured at the idea of a vision, but here, that seemed to be just another day's normal.

The young woman, Shelby, stood up, and her voice carried like a tune through the air. "I saw a tide—like the ocean, but brown red. It passed through our wood, filled our doorways, stoppered our mouths. It kept pouring in, closing off every portal until all of us were left breathless."

I leaned over to Jed. "I don't know geography very well, but there's not water big enough to bring that kind of mud near here, is there?"

"No—"

"The vision is not literal." LaKeemba was looking right at me. I never did whisper well. "It's figurative."

Jed gave me side-eye as if to say, "Seriously, you thought there was going to be a real flood." Color flooded my cheeks.

"The vision is not literal, but the way to stop it is. We have to build a net to catch what is wscoming."

I kept trying to figure out how a net was going to catch mud, but I soon gave up. I never was good about metaphors, not even when Jed was studying them in fifth grade English and left his textbook so I could read it at night.

"A magic net," Jed's voice rang out like a bell. "Something that will allow our magic to get out, but the uglier magic to stay out."

"Exactly, Jed." LaKeemba was smiling at him, and my cheeks flushed again, this time with pride. That's my boy.

"This is why you are here." LaKeemba was looking not just at Jed now, but at me too. I wanted to scoot away and out of sight. But given the work it took to get down here, it wasn't going to be pretty if I had to scooch my butt across the grass into the woods.

"You two must gather what we need. It is a journey only you can take. And you must complete it as quickly as possible."

Jed nodded, and I was pretty sure he was going to say, "Okay, so what do we do?"

But I put a hand over his mouth. "Wait a minute. You want the kid who didn't know he was magical until yesterday afternoon and the woman who—until seventeen minutes ago—no one could see, to go on a quest like in those fantasy books with the short people who have wide, hairy feet? Um, I don't think so. We're happy to help in any way we can from home, but nope, travel is not happening. Especially not time travel, if that's what you were thinking." Somehow, I'd gotten to my feet while delivering that speech, and I was feeling pretty good about myself until I looked over to see Jed's crest-fallen face.

LaKeemba said, "We make no one do the work. It is your choice, but we do need you."

Jed stood up next to me, and the boy looked like he might cry. I'd seen Jed cry a lot in private, but over the last six years, I could count on one hand the times he'd cried in front of someone other than me. I put my palm against his cheek. "Tell me."

"Mavis, I need to do this. I need to understand what I can do." A sob caught in his throat. Then, he looked me deep in the eye. "And I want to do this with you. For real. Where we work together, and everybody knows it."

When LaKeemba, Sharon, and Alonso had come back from the community center, Sharon had worked her magic and told the Wilsons that Jed had been accepted into an elite program and would need to go away for a while. He'd keep in touch via text but wouldn't be able to use the phone. He would be safe and would always have someone with him. I now realized that someone would be me. As much as I didn't want to go gallivanting all over God's green earth, I really didn't want that boy going alone, and I certainly didn't want to be a part of breaking a promise to the Wilsons—even if it was a promise I hadn't made. The Wilsons were good people, and they had raised a good son.

I turned to LaKeemba as we stood by the driveway that morning Jed found his drawing power, nodded, and said with as much solemnity as I could muster, "Show me your ways."

he titter of laughter that passed through the village children at my willingness to go died off only as they were shooed away to their huts. I knew I was going to make a fool of myself doing this quest thing. I didn't even have a sword or know a spell or even wear magic tennis shoes. But I was ready. If Jed was in, I was in.

So, we headed to LaKeemba's cabin, which was painted in bright ribs of color that had faded over time but still gave the house a festive, magical air. Her doorway was hung with strips of cloth that reminded me of the prayer flags that I'd seen on Mount Everest and on hippy houses on those HGTV shows the Wilsons watched at night.

Inside, the room smelled of something warm—like baking cookies abut woody and spicy—and the walls were covered with scraps of paper that showed sketches, all done in wide black swaths.

"Prophecies?" I asked, pointing to the wall.

LaKeemba smiled. "I'm trying to learn how to paint still life portraits. Those are my studies."

Were my cheeks ever going to return to their pasty white color again? I needed to stop talking.

"Please sit," Shelby said as she took a big cushion on the floor and pointed at a very comfortable-looking recliner and a straight-backed dining room chair. I'd be darned if I were going to take that old lady seat, so I plopped myself down in that dining room chair and instantly regretted it. It was the most uncomfortable seat I'd ever sat in.

Jed was leaning forward in the recliner, not even taking advantage of that cushioned back. "So, when do we leave?"

"Oh, slow your roll, dude," Sharon said as she came into the cabin. "First, you have to learn a few things."

"Spells. Potions. Incantations." Jed was literally bouncing on the edge of his very cushy seat.

Sharon's responding laugh sounded like a cookie cracking. "No. More like how to blend in. How to find things when you arrive. And how to call for help if you need it."

"Oh," Jed said, clearly disappointed.

"Ah, so like that show *Timeless*." As soon as I'd said it, I wished I'd listened to my earlier self and kept my mouth shut.

"Exactly. We don't have that budget or that wardrobe, but we can teach you a few tricks that will help you stick out less. You're already ahead of the rest of us, you being white and all. You won't draw as much attention wherever you go."

I had to admit that I hadn't thought of that. I hadn't thought of my whiteness. . . well, at all—ever. And I didn't quite see how that was going to be a factor here, but then Shelby said, "Remember that episode of *Timeless* where they go back to the 1920s and Rufus has to be extra careful?"

Suddenly, it made a lot more sense. Thank God for primetime TV.

"So, our whiteness is our shield, so to speak."

"Always has been, always will be, baby," Sharon said. "You'd be doing good to use it for something besides just yourselves, don't you think?"

I felt the color rise to my cheeks, but this time, it wasn't a little misspeak causing me to blush. This was guilt. Only my growing curiosity and interest in this journey kept me from blurting out something about how I hadn't gained anything by being white since no one but Jed could see me. I was right, but I held my tongue for once. Jed wanted this too badly for me to let my pride get in the way.

"Now, then," LaKeemba stepped out from behind what looked to be a quilt of fireplace screens that had been wired together to make a wall. "Let's get started."

For the next three days, those three women taught us how to change our voices to fit the times; the further back we went, the more formal our speech needed to become. No matter what, we were always going to be high-brow white folks since money got you almost as much access as white skin. They gave us a few pieces of clothing—vests and hats for Jed, a long skirt and a few hats for me. We would change based on the little booklet of images that Shelby had put together from historical photos on the internet. I didn't even ask how their access to Wi-Fi worked.

Then, the time travel training began. We didn't have a time machine, so we didn't need to worry about stashing it somewhere discrete. That was a load off my mind because, in *Timeless*, that seemed to be a major hindrance. But we did have to always find a big old tree of some sort, wherever we were. Hopefully, we'd be able to make our way back to the one we came in by, but if not, any tree that was at least three hundred years old would do.

I hadn't traveled much—okay, I hadn't traveled at all—but they didn't have to tell me that the closer we came to present day, the harder it would be to find an old tree. That part made me pretty nervous.

Our final lesson was about how we picked our time. We had to think about when we were going, and we both had to think about the same place, or we'd get separated.

"How'd I get here, then? I mean, I didn't even know you were here." Jed asked a good question.

"Ah, you were following Lizzie, and the two of you walk time better than most, so you just followed her trail in," Shelby said.

They made it sound so easy, but I wasn't stupid enough to think it was going to be that easy.

With our lessons in hand, they told us what we needed to find. I began to wish I'd watched more of *The Librarians* with Jed, instead of whining about how Noah Wyle would always be Dr. Carter to me and watching Jed roll his eyes because of my talk of "that old show" again.

This was going to be some quest.

6

*J*edidiah had always liked an adventure. Ever since I'd known him, the boy was forever begging someone to hide something so he could find it. He even had one of those talking books that said, "Find it," every time he opened the page. The book was broken and only worked on the zoo page, though. So eventually, Mrs. Wilson hid it in the trashcan under the paper towels she'd used to wash the day's eggs because she couldn't stand the roaring lion that actually sounded a lot more like it was passing gas. Luckily, Jed didn't go hunting in the trash. Well, at least not after his parents had put that latch on it.

The boy was just born looking for something, and the higher the risk, the more he wanted to hunt. His dad created elaborate scavenger hunts for him—hiding tools and candy all over the farm and then drawing crude maps for Jed to use to hunt down the goodies. Each time, as soon as he got back, Jed would sit and draw a better version of the map—a drawing made with pinpoint precision and drawn exactly to scale. Eventually, he would even do to-scale renderings of the farm from his gathered twigs. It was impressive.

For a while, he got into those video games that made him hunt down clues, but he solved those so quickly that his mom told him they couldn't afford to buy more games. He solved all the ones to rent at the Redbox, too, so his parents picked up a copy of *The Secret* from a used bookstore. Soon, he was lost in trying to figure out the cities and the clues using Google Earth. But when he started thinking about traveling to these places—at age eight—via digging in public parks, his parents took the book away.

Geocaching came next. Then, online scavenger hunts designed by artificial intelligence. Soon, Jed was writing his own online scavenger hunts and had hundreds of people playing them. If he hadn't been eleven—and, thus, subject to federal employment laws—he could have had a great career. But even that became boring for him.

So this—a real-life scavenger hunt through time and space—oh, the boy was veritably dancing in his shoes as we approached the pin oak.

"Jed, take a deep breath. We need to focus, remember?" I didn't want this child ending up in Timbuktu while I was in Detroit.

"Right. Okay." He raised his hands up by his sides and then dropped them as he exhaled. "Ready."

"We both have to be thinking about it as we cross, remember? So, what do you know?"

"The Kremlin. Lenin's tomb. St. Basil's. The Bolshoi."

"Good." I had to stop him, or he'd name every landmark in the city. "Think about those, and let's go." I wasn't about to admit that he was giving me my focus too. I just thought of those onion domes on that church, and off we went.

And there we were, right in Red Square—onion domes and all. Moscow, Russia. A place I never thought I'd see. Well, to be fair, I never thought I'd see the road in front of the Wilson farm, so this took the cake for best first road trip.

Jed was already walking across the plaza at lightning speed. When I finally caught up with him—it took a quick sprint from me—I had to stop him by grabbing his arm. "Jed, where do you think you're going?"

"Well, we have to find zveroboy, right? It's probably not going to grow in the city, so we need to head out."

I imagined the two of us walking the Russian countryside, passing wagons full of turnips and men in fur hats. My knowledge of 1920s Russia was very limited, but I still didn't like the image. "Whoa, Jed. Slow down. Let's make a plan. Maybe we can find some zveroboy already harvested and save ourselves a few days of work, huh?"

He raised his shoulders to his ears, and a wash of pink passed over his face as he grinned. "Oh, yeah, right. Sorry, I was doing it the way games require. There, you have to find the growing plant lots of times." He let out a long sigh. "But yeah, LaKeemba did say it just had to come from here in Moscow and that it didn't matter where we got it."

"Right, so let's ask someone about a tea shop. She said it's a tea, right?"

Jed nodded, and he headed toward a woman in a long camel-colored coat and a cloche. "Excuse me, miss. We're looking for a tea shop. My grandmother"—I wanted to throttle him as he pointed at me—"she's always wanted to try some zveroboy tea. Can you help us?"

The woman looked from Jed to me and back to him again. "Are you from America? You came a long way just for tea." She looked at me again. "How long was the sail?"

I stared blankly at her as I imagined the sailboats I'd seen on TV

—all white fabric and blue sea. But then I realized, we'd come back to 1924, just after WWI, and it wouldn't have been possible to fly here from the US, so I figured she meant one of those ships that people took big trunks on. "Oh, um, I sort of lost track. Several weeks." I sure hoped I was right. She didn't look surprised by what I said, so I figured I'd managed okay.

Jed shivered a little. The coat we'd brought—a simple black jacket that we hoped blended in—wasn't quite warm enough for an April day in Russia. The woman looked back at him, and her face softened. "Oh, you look like you could use a warm up. You just need to go around that corner." She pointed behind me to a small street that branched off the plaza. "There's a great little tea house a few doors down." She frowned. "But be careful. Too much zveroboy can be dangerous."

Jed nodded. "Okay, we will. Thank you, ma'am. Thank you." Suddenly, the kid had manners and a Southern accent as thick as mayonnaise. He sure knew how to pour on the charm.

Something about that woman was niggling at the back of my mind as we walked across the plaza. I couldn't put my finger on it, but something felt off.

While we looked for the shop, I tried to spot the things that let me know we'd gone back in time almost one hundred years. Most of the buildings looked like they'd already been around a few hundred years, so I figured they were probably the same even in 2019. The clothes were unusual to me, but I couldn't tell if that was the time difference, the country difference, or the fact that, besides the people I saw on TV—like that lady who wore the meat suit—I only knew what the Wilsons wore, which was mostly farm clothes.

To be honest, I couldn't have known we were in a different time at all, and Jed didn't seem to care a bit. He was far too focused on getting our "item," as he kept calling it, and getting back.

That was one of our rules. We had to bring each and every item back as soon as possible after we'd gotten it. LaKeemba said it was because they needed to start putting the magic net together immediately, but I also wondered if they thought it best not to have us running around the world and all of history with the stuff they needed, just in case something happened to us. I guess I could have been offended that they didn't trust us, but hey, we were a sixty-three-year-old woman who had been imaginary until a few days before and a twelve-year-old kid who had never been out of his home county except to go to the big city of Roanoke for birthday outings. I couldn't really blame them for their caution.

Just as the woman had said, there was a little tea shop. It said it right on the door. I almost thought nothing of that until I realized that I couldn't read Russian, and then I realized I couldn't understand it either. And yet, I'd understood the woman perfectly. That's what bothered me. I grabbed Jed by the arm again. "Wait! Can you read that?"

"Of course. It says, 'Mukolsikov's Tea Shop.'" He looked at me strangely as I stared at the words. "Oh, you must not have heard that part. That big dude—you know the guy with the giant hands—he worked a spell on us, so we can understand whatever people say no matter where or when we are. He said it was something like a 'Bable fish' from some old book I'd never heard of."

I hadn't ever heard of a Bable fish either, but the TARDIS did something similar. The Wilsons had seen every episode of *Doctor Who* several times, so I felt a bit like old hat. I was sure glad these magic people had done their thing. However, I was now a teensy bit nervous that I'd missed a whole bunch of stuff back when I'd been turning over the idea that I was real for the first time.

Jed pushed open the door of the shop and stepped in. It was

deliciously warm inside, and it smelled like campfire laced with peppermint and something like black licorice. Delicious.

"You better ask for the zveroboy. I don't think most kids in this time would have money to buy something."

I gave Jed a solemn nod—that kid was always thinking—and headed to the counter only to stop dead in my tracks. As I turned back to Jed, he whispered, "In your pocket." I slid my hand in, and there was a little purse full of money. I took it out and peeked in, trying to be slick and not look too much like I was surprised to find my pockets full of cash. The coins were all blank. I gave Jed another glance, and he did that waving motion that means "go on" no matter what language you speak.

The man behind the counter had a thick, wide moustache like the guy on the Pringles cans, and I had to stifle a giggle before I could say, "We'd like an ounce of zveroboy to go, please."

"To go?" the man said. "Ah, you mean to take home. Yes, yes, of course. One moment."

I glanced back at Jed, and he smiled from the corner he'd slid back into by the front window.

"Here you are." I turned back to the counter, and the man handed me a small paper bag. "That will be twelve rubles."

I opened the change purse and stared blankly at the coins.

"May I?" the man said. "I hear your accent. You are American, no?"

I nodded.

"Our money is new to you." He drew three coins out of the purse. "Perfect. Twelve rubles. Ten and two." He held each coin up in turn.

"Thank you," I said and picked up the small bag of tea before meeting Jed at the door and heading out.

"Well, that was easy," Jed said.

"Yep. This is going to be a piece of—"

The woman from the square was there, across the street. As soon as she saw me, she turned away as if pretending to look in the window of a butcher shop.

"What?"

"Oh, nothing. Let's go find our oak."

No need to alarm the boy, but I could feel my heart racing.

7

*W*e made it back to the village with no incident, and Jed rushed off to give the zveroboy to Sharon and Shelby. I caught LaKeemba's eye as we walked back into the village and gave her a nod. She quietly gestured toward her cabin, and I followed her in.

I had just opened my mouth to tell her about the woman when she said, "They found you already. I was afraid of that."

"Already? Wait! What? You knew people—People are follow— You didn't tell—" I took a deep breath. "Let me get a whole sentence out here. People are following us; you knew they were following us; and you didn't tell us?" I had my hands on my hips, and I could feel my chin jutting out past my chest.

LaKeemba gestured toward one of the big bean bag pillow things, but I refused. I was mad, and I wanted to show it.

She barely shrugged and sat down nimbly, like she did yoga every day and only ate kale. I kind of hated her in that moment.

"Jedidiah told you about David Poke?"

"The white guy who thinks he owns you all?"

"Right. Well, he's a traveler too."

"What? Jed told me that he couldn't come into our time. Said he was safe as long as he was back where? When? Whatever. Back on the farm."

"He is. You both are. Poke can't travel himself anymore. Shelby took care of that."

I had about a million questions about exactly what Shelby had done, but I had to focus here. "So, since he can't travel, he has a team of people who do it for him?"

"Exactly." LaKeemba took a sip out of a big ceramic mug of something so hot I could see the steam coming off of it. She poured another mug full and offered it up to me. I was so cold, so I took it and collapsed onto one of the bean bags, surprised that I didn't scald myself with the tea.

"We knew they were out there. Our people have seen them around. When you move through time and place as much as we do, you get good at noticing patterns and faces. When we saw the same person three or four times in three or four countries and time periods, we started to get the picture." She took another sip. "But it wasn't until Poke tried to threaten us with his team of spies that we knew he was behind it all."

"Threaten you? How could he threaten you? You all can travel through time? What can he possibly hold over you?"

A quietness settled on LaKeemba's face then, and she suddenly looked ten years older. "Our children."

I sputtered on my sip of tea. "I'm sorry, what?"

"Poke uses our children against us."

"I'm sorry. I don't understand." The air in the cabin suddenly felt very heavy, and part of me just wanted to get up, find Jed, and leave forever. This was bad. I knew it, and I didn't even know what *it* was.

LaKeemba let out a long sigh. "Some of our children can't travel. So, they stay here—always with one or two of us. But Poke knows that if something were to happen to most of us, our children would be vulnerable. That's why we have this village here, why we've settled."

I felt like I might throw up. "So, he is holding some of your children captive? Like slaves?"

"Not *like* slaves, Mavis. They *are* slaves. He had a man who works for him take them to a slave auction down in Richmond when those things were still happening, and then he pretended to buy them. So now, he has papers that say they belong to him. We can't disappear unless we want to leave them behind."

"And no one wants to leave their children behind. No one wants to abandon a child." I wanted to cry because I knew, without asking, that LaKeemba's child was one of these children.

"She's four. Mercy is her name." She and I walked to the cabin door, and she pointed. There, playing hopscotch with two other girls, was a small girl in a pink dress. Two braids hung down her back. She had her mother's way—solemn and focused.

"And she can't travel with you?"

"Not yet. Not yet." Her voice got soft then, and we sat silently in the darkening day.

"So, this net?"

LaKeemba gave her head a little shake. "We aren't sure yet. All we know is that our seers know something bad is on the way. It's likely Poke is involved, but we're not sure yet. And even if we were, we can't let him know we know."

A sliver of dread slid behind my shoulder blade. "Uh oh."

Her head snapped up. "What?"

"Before we knew who she was, we asked Poke's woman about the zveroboy."

A little color washed out of her face. She took a deep breath. "Okay, so that's not good, but we just need a good cover story." She stood up and moved toward the door. "And she doesn't know you are with us, right?"

I thought a moment. "I don't know how she could know."

"Okay, good. Come on. We need to make a plan."

I followed her out the door, and we headed across to Sharon's cabin. Shelby was standing at a tall table with a mortar and pestle at hand as she crushed what I assumed was the zveroboy into a fine green powder.

"Almost done," she said to LaKeemba as we came in.

"Okay, good. Keep working, but we also have to talk." She looked over at Jed. He was sitting in the corner with Lizzie, who was apparently teaching him how to shoot marbles. "Jed, you mind going to get Alonso?"

Jed looked up at her and then glanced at me. I gave him a nod. He stood and headed out. Good kid.

"Mavis, tell Shelby and Sharon what you just told me."

I told them about the woman, about asking her about the tea. They looked grave but not distraught, so I decided I'd take the same tack.

"Sounds like we need a diversion," Sharon said just as Jed and Alonso came in the room.

"A diversion. Like a distraction. I'm great at those. One time, during this hunt for the grail, I was in Egypt, and I saw—"

"Jed, I don't think everyone here needs to hear about your video game escapades," I said with a bit too much of a parenting tone even for my taste. Jed's face fell.

"No, let me hear, Jed." Sharon gave me a smile and then sat down beside Jed.

His voice was quiet at first. "So, this one group was trying to find the hieroglyph that had been added to Ramses II's tomb, because supposedly the Knights Templar had hidden a clue there during the Crusades." As he talked, his hands began to fly around his head, and he was soon standing up and gesticulating wildly as he told about how his team had created a false legend —a story about a papyrus scroll that had been snuck into Cleopatra's tomb—to confuse and distract the other teams on the hunt. "Soon, everyone was looking for our lie, and we were the only ones looking for the hieroglyph."

"That's genius, Jed." Alonso gave the boy a high five, and I thought Jed's face might break from his smiling. "So, what we need is a credible story that these two can spread about why they're hunting these particular things?"

"Leave the story to Jed and me," I said. "We'll work it up tonight, huh, Jed?" Alonso was grinning at me now.

"Sure will."

"Okay, good plan. You two get the story together. Jed, I trust you know the right places to leak a false lead, just like you would on your hunts." LaKeemba looked at Jed.

"Yep."

"All right, you two go with Alonso, but be careful. Poke's got people everywhere."

I followed Alonso back toward the oak and wondered if the expression "pig in a poke" was around yet.

---

8

*T*he next trip around the tree brought us to a city street. Alonso had told us to think about that show *Friends*. I'd had to remind Jed it was the "smelly cat" show, and then he was on it. He used to sing that song all the time when he was about five. Drove his mama crazy.

I figured that meant we were in New York, which seemed right given the massive number of cars and the super-tall buildings, but I didn't have much time to ponder because as soon as we began walking, Jed stopped cold. I looked over at him, and his eyes were as big as saucers.

"What, Jed?" I knew better than to touch him or step in front of him when he got like this. He was seeing something. Something we couldn't see.

Alonso looked at me, and I said, "The sight." Alonso nodded. We gently took up places next to Jed to give him a little space from the people streaming around us on the sidewalk, which was next to the park where we'd entered.

Jed began walking slowly. I tried to follow his gaze, but there were too many people, so I just stayed close beside him. The boy didn't even blink, just kept walking slow and steady. Soon, I was able to see that there was one other person walking at the pace we were. She was pushing a very full shopping cart. I could see a computer monitor sticking out—one of the old, boxy ones—and a lot of wires. She also had a fair amount of tinfoil on her body and in the cart itself, and she kept adjusting her knit cap. Each time, I'd catch a glimpse of foil by her ears.

We followed her for several blocks and turned a corner only to run right into her around the building. "Why are you following me?" Her voice was clear and bright.

I felt like my heart was going to jump out of my chest, Alonso had his fists raised, but Jed smiled and said, "You need us."

"I don't need you, boy. Go on." But she didn't sound convincing. In fact, she sounded like she was just saying something that she was supposed to say but meant the opposite.

"Yes, you do. We're not the only ones following you, and you need us."

"How do you know about them?" The woman dropped an elbow onto her shopping cart like she was too tired to stand up all the way anymore.

Jed smiled and glanced at Alonso and me. "They're following us, too."

The woman took off her hat then and sat down. She looked younger without the dusty pink cap and the tinfoil, maybe in her thirties. "How long they been onto you?"

"Just a day, not even. But they've been following our friends for longer. Why are they after you?" Jed took a seat on the lid of a trash can, and I couldn't help but think about how much I'd want to get those jeans washed right away.

The woman let out a long sigh. "Name's Hester." When I snickered a bit, she said sharply, "Yep, like that old book. My mom was a reader, blast her."

I had "borrowed" the book from Mrs. Wilson a few years back because I kept hearing people talk about it on PBS when I'd watch TV with the Wilsons after Jed went to bed. It was really good, if a bit slow.

But Jed had no idea about *The Scarlet Letter*. They didn't teach that in sixth grade English—too much innuendo. He just smiled and said, "Nice to meet you, Hester. I'm Jed. This is Mavis and Alonso."

"Nice to meet you all." She gave us a cursory glance and returned her gaze to Jed. "Well, they're following me because of this." She held out her hand, and in it was a quill pen. At least I thought that's what it was. It looked like something Nathaniel Hawthorne would have used to write *The Scarlet Letter*.

"Ah, I see. May I?" Jed gestured toward the pen, and when Hester nodded, he picked it up and held it out. "So, it writes the truth?"

"It does. You'd be surprised—well, maybe *you* wouldn't—how many people would prefer their lies to the truth."

"Doesn't surprise me at all!" I couldn't help but say.

"No, but then imaginary people know just how much people prefer to pretend they know everything." She didn't look at me when she spoke, but I could tell she was watching me from the corner of her eye.

"How did you?— Never mind." I had to stop trying to figure out how people knew so much about me. If Jed could do it, they could too, I supposed.

"So, yeah, I keep seeing these people no matter when I am. Same folks. A woman in a long coat. A kid with one lens in his broken glasses. A man with a cane that he doesn't even use."

"Oh yeah, we met the woman yesterday." Jed didn't seem fazed by our encounter, but just the memory of that woman gave me the willies.

"Steer clear of her. She's the worst. Tried to tie me to a street lamp one day."

I puzzled at that a moment. What exactly would be the good in tying someone to a street lamp?

Hester must have seen my befuddlement because she said, "She also tied raw steaks to me and then let the dogs from the neighborhood fighting ring loose."

I shuddered.

"Yep. She's something. That's when I started with all the tinfoil. Doesn't do a bit of good, but it helps me blend in, become almost invisible. Kind of like you, huh, Mavis?"

I just stared at her and wondered if her tinfoil hat was actually just for show. She sounded a little, well, off. Invisible, what was she talking about?

"What are they after you for?" Hester asked.

Jed crinkled his brow. "I don't really know, to be honest. We just got into all this yesterday."

"He's a truth-teller too," Alonso said. "Only pictures, not words."

"Ah, right. Got it. Okay, so why are you here? What do you need?"

Jed started to say something, but Alonso cut him off. "An internet café. We need to do a bit of business."

"Follow me." And off we went, Hester's shopping cart leading us all. I tried not to think about how odd we all looked walking down the street: a black man, an old, white woman, a middle-aged, white woman, and a white boy. But then, it was New York City, so maybe we didn't look odd at all. Maybe we just looked like family.

At the café, Alonso paid for our time at the computer, and Jed got to work, albeit more slowly than he was used to given that we were, in fact, in the late 1990s and dial-up was still the main way to get online. He kept starting to swear, but then, he'd cut his eyes at me and say, "Doggone it." It made me smile.

He was done soon enough, and when we all got back outside, where Hester was waiting for us, he said, "Story seeded. Now we wait."

"Good thing you're done," Hester said. "Saw that weird kid a few minutes ago. I led him around a while and lost him a few blocks back, but you best be on your way. Nearest tree is just around the corner in the park."

Jed gave Hester a quick hug. "Thanks, Hester. Nice to meet you. You know how to get me if you need us, right?"

"Sure do." She gave me a wink and said, "You take care of him, Mavis. He's special."

"Don't I know it," I said. I had no idea how Jed would get her message, and I didn't ask. I was finally learning. I sure hoped she'd be okay. She seemed like good people.

We found Hester's tree easily enough and just in time because as we slipped around it, I saw the boy with the broken glasses step around the corner.

JEDIDIAH

I know Mavis makes me out to be some kind of computer genius, but let's remember: she has only ever talked to me. I may have misled her about my skills a bit. Sure, I could geocache, and I was pretty good. And I could beat Zelda with my eyes closed, but those nineties games are so lame anyway.

But the internet stuff. . . Mavis is just impressed by Google.

I did know how to leave a false trail in a game, of course, but in real life, I was just tossing things out. I got on Tor—the dark web browser my parents scrupulously deleted in their nightly computer check—at the internet café. I had to hack into some Navy servers, but that was pretty simple. I couldn't believe Tor even existed back then—back before I was alive—but there it was in a much more code-heavy version than I was used to, but still the same Tor.

I created a quick website with some information about these people with abilities, like on that show **Heroes** *that my mom liked so much because of some guy named Milo. I made a whole bunch of posts about sightings and asked for people to tell me if they'd seen folks like this too. I acted both scared and fascinated—which wasn't much of an act—and then I posted it with the codename Simon Prowls. I don't know where I* *came up with that, but it sounded both like a fake name and yet adult enough to be feasible.*

It wasn't really that fancy, especially given how slow *that internet connection was, but I hoped it would be enough.*

Then, that kid showed up as we were getting out of there, and I began to worry that I hadn't logged out of everything. I hoped I had.

And I hoped Hester would call me if she needed me. She was in danger, and she knew it. She tried to act all cool, but I could see she was terrified. It was on her like bad cologne. I'd have to keep an eye out for her call.

9

*J*ed had always been special. I know, everyone says that about the kid they love best, but I don't mean that he was kind or smart or could throw a baseball at three days old. None of that braggy stuff.

I mean, he's really special. For instance, when he was five months old, his mom arranged a playdate for him because she was worried that her baby had never seen anyone but his parents. When the little girl came over, she was screaming so hard that she could barely breathe. Her mom said something about a sleep regression—whatever that was. But when her dad set her down on the blanket next to Jed, she stopped crying immediately. She and Jed just lay there looking at each other for the whole hour.

That kind of special.

Or when this big kid was bullying a girl in Jed's kindergarten class, he took the big kid aside and asked him, "I can see that big bruise on your side. That must hurt."

The kid just looked at him and nodded.

"You get that from your dad?"

The kid nodded again.

"I'm sorry. Should I go with you to tell the principal?"

Another nod, and the two of them walked off to the principal's office together. The kid never bullied anyone again, not once he got to live with his mom.

See? Special.

So, part of me wasn't really surprised by the fact that Jed had found these magic people, and I certainly wasn't surprised that he was one of them. I was still getting used to everyone being able to see me; that was weird, and I wasn't sure I liked it. But when I saw Jed's face and watched him bounce on his heels each time we came around that tree back into the village, I decided to pull up my big girl panties and deal.

I knew Jed was tired of being special. He just wanted to be normal, to not have to be the one to fix things or be sympathetic to the people others couldn't stand. It was hard for him to always be the one giving the compassion, never the one getting it.

I always figured that's why I was around. Okay, and *how* I happened to be around was something I chose to just leave as a mystery. My job—my only job in the whole world—was to take care of Jed so that he could take care of other people.

Now, though, Jed didn't need me in the same way. He had other people watching out for him, other people who knew he was special but didn't need him to be. Part of me thought it would be better for me to just leave him there in Heavenland and go on about my way, but I had two reasons not to. First, I had no idea what "my way" was without Jed. And secondly, at night, Jed sat with me by the fire and sometimes put his head in my lap so I could play with his hair. Those minutes. . . Those were worth the whole day of feeling a bit useless and lost.

Soon, though, my role became much more important, more important even than being a little boy's best friend.

THE STORY JED had sent whizzing around the internet took root fast. The villagers were coming back from their own trips with stories about people who could scale the sides of buildings and summon a magical hammer. I didn't know the Marvel universe that well, but even I knew about Spider-Man and Thor, but people will believe anything if it seems secret enough. I had to admire Jed's use of his extensive comic book collection.

Soon, he and I were making trips to pick up the ingredients for the net without seeing any of Poke's people. We visited Porbandar in India—where Gandhi was born—and got a special blend of curry that a monk carried in a pouch on his belt. Then, we headed to Brazil and picked up, very carefully, a spider whose venom could kill a grown man in five minutes. (I let Jed carry the glass jar with that guy. My protective side had its limits, and those limits had eight legs.) We hit Seattle to get a piece of green chewing gum off that weirdly fascinating but totally disgusting gum wall near the Pike Place Market. And our last stop was in Paris to gather a bit of ash from the fire that had so ravaged the Notre Dame Cathedral. All our ventures were easy and pretty cool. While Jed did see several magic people on our travels, he didn't feel compelled to meet any of them, which was just as well because we were in a hurry.

After our final trip, we came around the oak only to find a crowd of people with their backs to the tree. It looked like everyone in the village was there, standing very close together right where we needed to walk. I was just about to do the good old "excuse me" push and shove when Lizzie wiggled through a pair of legs and whispered, "Poke's here. We've been causing a scene to keep y'all safe. But he's starting to get suspicious, so you need to go. Now."

Jed and I looked at each other and nodded. "The farm," Jed mouthed, and we stepped back around the tree and into the forest behind the barn. I could hear Mr. Wilson working in his shop, and Jed must have heard him, too, because he gestured for me to keep low. We snuck past the windows and into the front of the building before climbing the old ladder to the hayloft. Jed wasn't due back to the farm for quite some time, and while I knew that Sharon had worked her magic, I wasn't sure how sturdy that excuse would be if we showed up unexpectedly.

For a good while, we just sat up there quietly, enjoying the bird sounds and the off-key singing of Mr. Wilson. The man was a die-hard Tom Petty fan.

Tthen, Jed looked at me. "Can I ask you something?"

"Anything."

"Do you think Hester is okay?"

It took me a minute to remember the woman we'd met in New York a few days back. We'd seen a lot of people in our travels. "I suspect so. Why do you ask?"

"Well, you said that the kid that works for Poke saw us, right? Do you think he saw us with Hester? Did we get her into some trouble?"

A chill passed over me, but I said calmly, "Hester's been taking care of herself for a long time, Jed. I expect she's just fine."

"You expect or you know?"

"Well, of course, I can't be sure—"

"We have to go. Now. She needs us." Jed already had his feet on the ladder.

"Jed."

He was gone down into the barn below.

"Crap." I lumbered down the ladder with the grace of a pregnant elephant on a ladder and followed him back into the woods to the tree. He paused long enough to say, "New York, 1996, right?" and see me nod. Then, he was off with me right behind him.

We came out at Hester's tree this time. We were dressed a little oddly since we'd been in Victorian-era Paris earlier that day, but in New York, weird is very relative, so no one paid us much mind.

Jed started to rush off down the street, but I grabbed him by the arm. "Jed, wait. What is going on?"

"Hester called."

"You don't even have a phone."

He gave me a look of frustration that could wither a charging tiger. "She reached out, you know, through the. . . Oh, I don't know how to explain it. I just know she needs us."

I was totally confused by what Jed was saying, but I trusted him. If he said we needed to find Hester, we needed to find Hester. Only one problem: I had no idea how to go about finding anyone in New York, much less someone who didn't even have an address. Good thing what I knew didn't seem to matter. Jed had headed up the street at almost a jog, so I figured he had some sort of magic people homing beacon or something. I had to run to catch up. It wasn't pretty.

We moved down the sidewalk as quickly as we could for several blocks, but then Jed stopped and looked back at me, a wash of horror on his face. "Hurry."

I hope the good Lord will forgive me, but my first thought was, "Not more running." But Jed was sprinting away, so I dug deep, hiked up my long skirts, and took off after him.

He was just turning a corner up ahead, and I was swinging around the brick building to follow him when I stopped cold. There, in a heap with all her earthly possessions around her, was Hester. She could have been sleeping, but the ghastly pallor on her skin told me she was dead. Jed was standing over her, tears streaming down his face, so I walked over and laid my hand on her cheek. She was still a bit warm. Having watched too many police shows, I knew this meant she hadn't been dead long.

"We have to go, Jed." I grabbed his hand and tried to pull him back out of the alley, but he stood fast and almost jerked my arm out of the socket. "Jed. Now."

"She's empty." I barely heard him. "Just empty."

I stepped between him and Hester's body. "Yes, Jed. That's just her body now. Hester isn't here."

He blinked and looked up at me then. "Where did her magic go?"

I tilted my head. "What do you mean? She died. She doesn't have magic anymore."

"I know that," he snapped. "But her magic has to go somewhere. Where did it go?"

I was thoroughly confused, but the knife wound in Hester's chest, the one I was hoping Jed wouldn't see, didn't bode well for us, so there was no time to figure out what he meant. "Jed, we have to go."

Just then, a tall thin man with a cane stepped into the head of the alley. "What's your hurry? Maybe I can answer some of Mr. Wilson's questions?"

Never before had I wished I'd known karate, but man, I wanted to kick somebody in the teeth. He just stood there, so smug and relaxed.

"Who are you?" My voice was sharp and high.

"Oh, I'm Mr. Glass. I believe you know my associate, Mr. Poke."

I was just about to play dumb when I felt Jed's hand grab mine and heard him say just above his breath, "On three. One, two, three."

And then, suddenly, we were on the other side of Mr. Glass and turning into the bookshop two doors up the street we had just run down. As we entered the store, I glanced back and saw Mr. Glass standing there, his mouth moving like he was still talking.

We slid to the back of the shop—to the cozy children's section that had a mural of the tree in one corner—and lowered ourselves to the brightly colored pillows there. Jed picked up a copy of *Percy Jackson* and held it open like he were reading.

"That should hold for a few minutes. Long enough for them to think we are far away."

I dropped my chin. "Jedidiah Wilson, what did you do?"

"Oh, just a little mirage. Lizzie taught me how."

"A mirage? Like that man thinks we're still standing there."

"For a few minutes. Not long enough for us to make it to the tree though. So, I thought we might fool them by not running."

"You have played too many video games, son." I wanted to sound stern, but mostly, I was just so proud. "So, now you can do magic, too, huh?"

"Always have been able to, Alonso says. Just needed a reason to figure out how."

"Staying alive is a pretty good reason."

He nodded and then began to read for real.

*a*fter a few moments of shock and catching my breath, I knew we had to make a move. We asked the bookshop clerk where the best park in the city was, and after a very noticeable eye roll, she told us, "Central Park." I almost rolled my eyes too because even I knew about Central Park.

"Are there big trees there?" Jed put on the wide-eyed gaze of a very innocent twelve-year-old, and I saw the girl visibly soften toward him.

"Yeah, there are. A really pretty grove of elms. But, if you're looking for the coolest big tree around," the woman's voice glittered with excitement, "you need to go see the hangman's elm in Washington Square."

"People were hung there?"

"No, not really. That's just an old legend. It used to be on a farm, and for whatever reason, it just never got cut down. Now it's protected."

Jed looked at me, and I smiled. "Guess we're going to Washington Square Park," I said.

"Oh, you don't really have to go anywhere." The almost eye roll was back. "It's across the street."

Sure enough, there was a park. In all our rushing and dodging, I hadn't even noticed.

"Thanks," Jed said over his shoulder as we headed for the door.

"No problem, Jedidiah," she said with a wink as she turned back to her desk.

I didn't even break my stride. "Another one, huh?" I was getting used to this.

"Yep."

"And you knew it?"

"Yep."

We reached the elm, and it was magnificent. A woman begins to appreciate trees when they are her only way home. This one was towering—which is saying something on the island of Manhattan —but also graceful, almost like she was swaying to the song of the wind. When we reached her, I placed my fingertips against her bark, and I could have sworn she vibrated beneath them.

I chalked the feeling up to too much woo-woo for one week and grabbed Jed's hand as we both thought of the village.

When we crossed over, the crowd was gone; Lizzie was there waiting for us at the tree and jetted off to LaKeemba's cabin as soon as we arrived.

Shelby got up from the fire with cups of water for us, and we both gulped down the cold drink as much to quench our fear as our thirst. "You met him?"

"How did you know?" I immediately felt stupid. Another dumb question.

But Shelby just smiled and said, "You have the look of it about you."

I really wanted to ask what that meant, but I held my tongue.

"A mirage?" she said to Jed.

"You can see it in my waves, huh?"

"Yeah, that's pretty big magic. Need some food?"

"Yes, please." And for the first time, I really looked at Jed and saw just how gaunt he had gotten over the past few days. I wasn't doing such a great job of looking after the boy. At the very least, I could have gotten him a slice of pizza while we were in the Big Apple.

He sat down with Lizzie and ate a big bowl of beef stew. I picked at mine, but my appetite was mostly gone. I couldn't get Mr. Glass's face out of my head. He had looked something like a combination of Snape and the way I pictured Gollum—sort of greasy and shifty. I shuddered.

"He's scary. No doubt about it." Alonso had dropped down beside me on my log.

"Who?" I was getting tired of people knowing what I was thinking.

"Glass." Then he laughed. "I've met him, too, and he is terrifying.."

The fact that Alonso had known I was thinking about Glass creeped me out in a major way, but I was up for commiseration in whatever way it came. "Sure is. The way he talked—like he had it all figured out and we were just going to do whatever he wanted."

"Privilege. The reek of privilege."

"I was going to call it 'being a big jerk,' but you use whatever word you want."

Alonso let out a huge chortle that seemed to shake the trees, and I thought of the elm back in Washington Square Park. "So, the trees?"

"Ah, they're starting to talk to you, huh?"

Again, with the mind reading. "Um, sort of. The one we came through in New York. She was sort of humming when I touched her."

"Oh yes, they dance and sing a lot. All those naiad and dryad myths came from somewhere."

"So, can they talk and walk?"

Alonso smiled. "No, Tolkien went a little far with the Ents. The trees I know don't walk or talk, but they do help, usually with moral support. But I have known a great one or two to drop a limb at just the right moment."

I smiled. I liked knowing I lived in a world where even the plants worked for good.

I was about to ask Alonso what other supposedly insentient creatures could actually feel and move, but LaKeemba came out of her cabin then, and she didn't look happy. In fact, she looked almost scared, and LaKeemba scared was not a thing I ever wanted to see.

"Friends," she said to the crowd that had instinctively gathered. "The net is in place, but we must still be vigilant. Jed and Mavis had a close call today. It was only Jed's quick thinking that saved them."

A flush came to my cheeks. Again, I was failing that boy. Not only was I not protecting him, he was having to protect me.

"And now Poke knows that we have help here." She looked at me then. "White help. And white help is dangerous. Always has been."

"So, what are we going to do?" Alonso said.

"We're going to keep to the plan. We're almost there. So, we keep going."

"Even though Poke is threatening to sell the kids away?" A young woman, maybe twenty-five, asked as she crouched by the fire.

"Even though," LaKeemba said.

I looked from the young woman to LaKeemba and then over at Jed. He gave me a small shake of his head—maybe to tell me he didn't understand or maybe to suggest I not say anything, but he should have known that I wasn't going to keep my mouth shut.

"I'm sorry. I thought the plan was finished now. The net is up. The evil is kept out. The village is safe, which means you all can stay here, and your kids are safe, too."

A big sigh passed through the villagers. Only later would I realize the sigh wasn't one of frustration, not completely anyway. No, their breath was carried by weariness, by the fatigue of having to help people understand for so long.

Shelby stepped forward then. "The plan is for us to escape, Mavis. All of us, including the children."

I looked at her closely, and for once, I didn't say the first thing that came to mind. But I was confused. They had a place to live, the ability to travel anywhere in the world, powers that let them do amazing things. What more could they want?

"You understand, don't you, Jed?" LaKeemba had walked over and knelt down in front of him.

He nodded slowly, and then he looked at me. "They want free-dom, Mavis. We know what that's like, right? To not be able to be who we are completely, to not be able to live the way we want to because of what people might say, what people might do."

I felt it then—the lightning bolt of shame that brings understanding. I did know. For all of the twelve years I'd been aware of being alive, I'd been tied to the Wilson farm, to Jed. I hadn't ever known any different, so I hadn't really thought about wanting different. But now, now that I knew what it was to go wherever I wanted, to eat, to be seen. . .

"What do we need to do?" I was standing up, and once again, I didn't even know how I'd gotten there.

JEDIDIAH

When I saw Mavis standing there, her hands on her hips like she was the old white Wonder Woman, I felt this strange mix of pride and terror. I scrambled up to stand beside her. Mavis was my best friend, and I loved her. But really, I just wanted my mom. That's not something a twelve-year-old can admit though. I had to put on a good face.

Still, we stood there and waited for LaKeemba and Shelby to tell us what to do; I imagined myself at the breakfast table at the farmhouse. I sat in my seat by the window where I could see the goats and the Great Pyrenees dogs. Mom had made my favorite breakfast of dippy eggs and slightly burned bacon, and Dad was over-the-top laughing because he knew it would make me laugh.

After breakfast, Dad put me on the tractor to mow the fields, and I could see Mom out there in the garden, hoeing up all the tiny weeds. "You got to get them when they're little, Jed. That's the easiest time." She must have said that to me a thousand times by now.

Dad was in his workshop, tinkering on his old Jeep again. "Your Jeep," he always said to me, to which I would smile, feel all warm, and wish for my brand-new Jeep Gladiator. He used to do the mowing, but he knew how much I liked it. He always made me wear the seatbelt and *keep the roll bar up. Some folks thought twelve was too young for mowing, but Grandaddy starting plowing—which was a lot harder, let me tell you—when he was just nine. So, I was late to the game, as far as he was concerned.*

We'd go in at noon and eat lunch, this time sandwiches Dad had put together. (My parents were big on making sure I knew there was no such thing as men's jobs and women's jobs. "Just jobs that need doing," Dad said.) Then, I'd curl up with a book between the hound dogs on the couch and read until I took a nap. . .

I was smack dab in the middle of that nap when I heard my name. I wiggled my head to clear the sleep away and found myself curled up with my head in Mavis's lap and LaKeemba sitting over me.

Talk about embarrassing. What a baby thing to do—to fall asleep right in the middle of the big plan. I wanted to get up and shake it off like I'd fallen asleep on purpose, but then, I felt it. It was out there in the dark beyond the campfire, held back by the net, but eager to get in. . . And angry. Oh, so angry.

I kept my head in Mavis's lap and hoped it would go away.

11

*T*urned out, I didn't really know what I was getting in to. And it took LaKeemba and Shelby a long time to catch me up.

As soon as I volunteered, the two women took my arms and herded me toward LaKeemba's cabin. I peeked back over my shoulder and saw Jed and Alonso following behind. Soon, we were all on cushions on the floor, Jed right next to me. He looked so tired, so I put my arm around his shoulders and eased his head down to my lap. Then, I played with his hair. Soon, I felt the rhythm of his breath deepen. He was asleep.

While he dozed, the three villagers told me about Poke, about how he had won members of the village over at first by bringing gifts of lumber, seeds, and even animals to help them get established. He acted like he thought they were runaway slaves—"He had me believing too," Shelby said—and pretended like he was an abolitionist. He kept talking about "the railroad" and acting like the villagers should all know what it was.

LaKeemba laughed. "That was the funny part, of course, because we'd all heard of the Underground Railroad, but none of us were on it. Heck, most of us were born in the twentieth century when trains were so normal that we almost didn't notice them at all. So, when he kept talking about 'the railroad,' most of us just thought of train tracks. We didn't really play along very well." She paused. "The way he overlooked our slip-ups should have been our first clue."

Apparently, Poke played this game just long enough to find out who had children and figure out how the villagers could help him. Then, he made his move.

"We had tried hard not to let him know we was magical." Sharon had stepped into the cabin. "But it's hard to be something you're not, especially when people is hurting." Her face was pained. "He figured it out—figured out what most of us could do. That's when he had us."

"But he knew more than we accidentally showed him, too. We've never really figured out if 'it'"—LaKeemba swung her hand wide over her head—"is his pet or his master, but 'it' tells him things."

"It? What is it?"

"That's the thing," Shelby said. "We don't know. The net is keeping It out, now that it's back."

I shuddered. I didn't like faceless monsters. They were always scarier than the ones you could identify, at least in movies. "You just called it, um, 'it'? Like the Stephen King movie?"

Sharon nodded. "We're open to suggestions."

"What if we called it Bartholomew?" I suggested. "I've never thought a Bart could be that scary."

"All I can picture is Bart Simpson," Alonso said.

"See? It's working already," I said.

LaKeemba wasn't smiling though. "One night, he showed up with four big men, and I knew instantly that they were magic too. I could feel it coming off of them in waves, but not like waves I'd want to step into. More like waves I knew I needed to brace against."

"The men bound the villagers to their cabins, and then Poke walked through each and every door where there was a child who didn't have magic and took them right away from their parents."

"Mercy too?" I asked in a hushed voice.

LaKeemba nodded, and I saw her hand go to her belly. I couldn't even imagine. "The next day, he sold them to himself, and now, we can't run."

"Not yet." Sharon's voice was steely.

"Not yet." LaKeemba set her gaze on Jed. "That boy is strong, but just as well, it's better that he not hear all of this."

I ran my fingers lightly through Jed's hair one more time, just to be sure he was asleep. "Tell me about the net."

LaKeemba nodded and stood up before she began to pace the room. "The net is partially protection, partially alarm. It will slow down something coming at us long enough for us to get away."

"Something? Or someone?" I could hear the waver in my voice.

"Something. Poke works with a force. We still don't know quite what it is, but it protects him. It seems to know when he's in danger."

"A force? Like *Star Wars*?"

This time, LaKeemba smiled. "Kind of, actually. It seems to give him warnings and things, but it's not neutral. It's definitely evil. Very evil."

A long silence settled in the cabin.

Then, Shelby leaned forward and picked up a piece of straw from the floor. "We've tried to get the children's papers before, but each time, it's ended badly."

"How badly?" I wasn't sure I wanted the answer, but I knew I needed it.

"Somebody died both times."

"What? How?"

"We don't know, Mavis," Shelby said.

I shuddered, but I could tell by the look on her face that I shouldn't ask for more information. "So, the net?"

All three women looked at me with open faces as if they wanted me to ask the question, so I obliged. "The net is going to let us know when Poke's thing arrives because we are going to lure it here while someone else gets the papers."

"Yes. And Mavis, this is where we need you." Alonso had been silent this entire time, but when he spoke these words, it was with authority. "You are our bait."

I almost laughed out loud as I imagined myself as a tiny minnow like the ones Jed used to catch trout in the pond below the farm-house. Lithe, thin, and oh, so wiggly. I was none of those things with my too-wide hips and achy joints. But I managed to keep my composure and say, "Ah, the old bait and switch again, huh? Seems like we're doing a lot of that these days."

Shelby smiled. "Ah, but this time, no computers." She gave me a wink.

I laughed. "Okay, first question. Does this require me to run?"

"No," Sharon said.

"Second, am I going to be in danger?"

Alonso answered this time. "Probably."

I took a deep breath and nodded. "Finally, can you promise me Jed will be safe?"

"Yes, and I can make that promise binding right now." LaKeemba looked me dead in the eye, expectation written into the lines of her face.

"Do it," I said. "Now." There was a firmness in my voice that I hadn't heard before, but I was more certain than I'd ever been about anything. I had to protect this child.

LaKeemba leaned forward and placed one hand on Jed's forehead and one on his right hip. She took a deep breath in, and then she exhaled gently from the top of his head to the bottom of his feet.

When she sat back, she looked tired, thinner almost.

"Thank you," I said as Jed stirred in my lap. "Thank you."

Jed sat up. "Oh no, I'm sorry I fell asleep. What did I miss?"

He looked me right in the face, and for the first time in his life, I lied. "Not much, baby. Just us telling stories."

LaKeemba looked at me and nodded.

12

The next morning after breakfast, Alonso took Jed on a trip for training. I knew that the trip was mainly a way to get Jed away while I actually prepared for my new role in this whole process, but Alonso had also promised me he'd actually give Jed some guidance on how to survive in a world that didn't really believe in magic and, thus, doesn't protect the good people who have it from the bad ones who do.

"Don't worry, Mavis. Jed is one of us. We will never love him as well as you do, but we do love him." Alonso wasn't a man of many words, but the ones he spoke rang big in my heart.

As soon as they turned around the tree, I headed for LaKeemba's cabin. She had lit candles on every surface, and the whole space smelled of cinnamon. "It smells great in here. Part of a ritual?"

She smiled. "I'm making stewed apples for our lunch."

I felt the color rise to my cheeks again.

She pointed to a chair by the window, and I took a seat. Then, she began the first makeover of my life. To start, she trimmed my silver hair and then twisted it expertly into an updo. When she gave me the small hand mirror, I almost didn't recognize myself. I looked more pulled together than I'd ever looked in the few times I'd bothered to look in a mirror. Yet, I looked reserved too —not flashy or flamboyant.

Shelby joined us then, and while LaKeemba gave me a manicure, Shelby braved the wastelands that were my neglected feet and gave me the best—and only—pedicure I'd ever had. I thought I could melt into the floor. It was only later that I realized they'd done this only out of care because no one else would ever see my feet.

While the other two women worked on my hands and feet, Sharon began to teach me a few basic phrases that would set me in good stead for my journey. She reminded me that white women were prized in the antebellum South, but not as equals, more as possessions. To blend in, I would need to carry myself well without drawing attention. I had to let myself be waited on by slaves (I cringed at the thought) but also by men who would want to hold the door for me and take care of me like I was a small sick child.

"Now, you can't make that face, Mavis. They'll find you out for sure if you do," Sharon scolded.

I tried to set my face into an expression akin to a paper plate, and she said, "Better."

When they felt like my body and speech were in good form, Shelby stepped out from behind the shutter-wall in LaKeemba's cabin with an armload of clothes. I could see that she was holding only dresses, and I groaned.

"I know, Mavis. You're not much of a long-skirt kind of woman. But girl, you've got to play the part. And if I do say so myself, I don't think those baggy, grandma jeans and t-shirts are doing you any favors. You've got a figure in there, and we need to see it." Shelby had a way of convincing a woman to do most anything.

I stepped back behind the shutters with Shelby and came out in a long blue dress that cinched tight at my waist. I'd convinced Shelby a corset would make me so uncomfortable that I wouldn't be able to stay in character, but she'd still pulled the laces tight enough on the dress to make me feel like I might never breathe again. The skirt fell almost to the floor over the top of little black boots with just a bit of a heel. Beneath the skirt, I felt like I was wearing an entire Christmas's worth of wrapping paper, but Shelby assured me that a proper woman always had some crinoline on to hide the shape of her legs. I felt ridiculous. And fussy. I didn't like fussy.

But I gathered from the smiles on the women's faces that I must look all right, and I found myself smiling a bit too. "Do you all ever dress up like this?"

The women looked at each other. "Not in this time, honey," Sharon said.

Color rose to my cheeks again. "I'm so stupid. Of course not." I remembered the pictures I'd seen of black women from slave days. They had worn much simpler, less formal dresses that were much like this one in shape but nothing like it in fashion.

"You're not stupid, Mavis. You're just not used to thinking from anything other than your own experience." LaKeemba's voice was kind but clear. "Most white people are like that. They think that their experience of the world is the normal way, and if someone has another experience, it's because that person is wrong. That's white supremacy."

Again, I felt color rise to my cheeks, but this time, it wasn't from embarrassment. It was anger. "I'm not a white supremacist."

LaKeemba spoke softly but clearly again. "No, Mavis. You're not, not in the way you think of with the hoods and the burning crosses. But as a white woman, even one almost no one could see until recently, you do get to place yourself in the system that favors whiteness. Black folks and other people of color, we've never been able to do that. We've always had to know how to work within the white system even as we knew we weren't part of it."

I took a long breath because as much as I wanted to argue, what she said made sense. "That's what that girl talks about in *The Hate U Give*, right? How at her school she's not really herself?"

"Look at you, Mavis, all up on the contemporary books about race. Yes, that's it exactly." Another gesture of Shelby's kindness.

Sharon sat down hard. "But Mavis, just because you isn't wearing a hood doesn't mean you don't get some of the benefits of white privilege. And just because you didn't choose it don't mean you don't get it either."

I looked at my friends—realizing just then that this is what these women had become to me—and I knew they were telling me the truth, trusting me enough to tell me. And I knew without a shadow of a doubt that they were doing me a kindness here, even though I still wanted to defend myself and say, "But I'm not racist."

This one time, though, I kept my thoughts to myself. I needed time to think all this over, and now was not the time. We had children to save.

"Okay, so can we go over the plan again?" I said.

"Right." Sharon stood up. "You is headed to Poke's place to inquire about buying some slaves."

I hated even the thought of pretending to do this, but I knew that my part was to pretend. It was a relatively easy part in that regard.

LaKeemba continued reviewing my backstory. "You have money because your father just died and left you, his only daughter and a widow, all of his inheritance. He was—"

"Courtney Wallace from Washersburg, Maryland. Right?"

"Right." Shelby was pulling the laces on my dress tighter again. "You are especially interested in a little girl to be a companion and house girl to your own daughter, Samantha."

I felt like I had my story down. "What if he recognizes me?"

"We're counting on the fact that he will," LaKeemba said. "You're the bait, remember? We suspect he'll have seen your picture; his people always take pictures. It's part of their insurance against us. But the clothes, demeanor, and request will probably give you enough access to the house and his files to see where the papers are before he susses out just what you're up to."

"Then, I lead him back here just to confirm what he already suspects?"

"Precisely. Damn girl, you'd make a great CIA operative." Shelby was grinning from ear to ear, but I could see the nervousness in her eyes.

I curtsied low and said, "I know, right?" I figured it was best to play along and pretend that I wasn't terrified too.

Sharon smiled and then led me toward the door. "You best be headed on then. Jed be back soon."

"What will you tell him?"

Sharon leaned against the door frame. "The truth. That his best friend is off to save us all."

I ducked my head to hide my blush and began my walk to Poke's plantation.

JEDIDIAH

I didn't know what Mavis and LaKeemba talked about while I slept, but the next morning when Alonso pushed so hard to get me to take a trip with him, I knew something was up. Adults always think kids don't know, but most of the time, we do. We may not know what, but we know something.

I saw Mavis at breakfast, and she looked excited and nervous—sort of keyed up over something—but she seemed happy to have me go with Alonso, so I went. I trust Mavis. If she says saying something is good, I know that it is.

Alonso told me to think of the Navajo Pueblos, those amazing houses built into the sides of cliffs, and then to picture them filled with people. I concentrated on the images I'd seen when we'd studied Mesa Verde in the sixth grade, and then we walked. As we came around what was actually a huge cactus, I lost my breath. There were the cave dwellings, and people were moving in and out of them just like they moved in and out Main Street in Homeover.

"Now, Jed, you get to really learn." Alonso's voice was hushed. "Today, you listen far more than you talk, okay?"

I nodded, and we began the climb up to the dwellings.

What I learned that day was special, too much to even try to wrap words around. I met people who were so powerful that the magic seemed to live in their bones. I met people who teased the magical people the way we tease those we love most. I met people who made food that burned the skin out of my throat but then cooled me down, so I felt restful and quiet.

Mostly, though, I met people who knew a ton, more than any of my teachers ever thought they knew. But no one was bragging there. By the end of the day, I began to wonder why we needed to tell everyone what we knew or thought or believed as soon as we knew it. I thought about maybe getting rid of my phone when I got home.

Maybe. It'd be hard to part with Instagram though.

By the time we got back to the village, I was so tired I could barely see straight, but I saw enough to know that Mavis wasn't there. And that woke me right up.

13

I've never been a woman for exercise. If it doesn't serve me the purpose of getting me somewhere I need to go, why in the world would I walk? And running? Ha! So, I wasn't at the peak of cardiovascular fitness. Add to that about eight billion pounds of fabric in my dress, and that stroll to Poke's plantation was miserable.

But my own pain soon slid aside as I walked past the people lining the drive, every one of them black, every one of them guarded. I could see it in their posture—the way they looked at me (but not directly) and kept hoeing while also rotating to keep their faces toward me as I passed.

I so very much wanted to wave, at least, or to walk over and introduce myself. "Hi, I'm Mavis, and LaKeemba sent me." Not only would doing that blow my cover, but it would probably put them in a lot of danger, too. I just kept my face steady and my gaze straight ahead.

I could see the big house there ahead of me, straight on down the lane lined with cedars on both sides. This was an entrance like something from a movie. I could almost picture the opening shot: a camera flies in from among the tree branches and then zooms toward the house, stately and grandiose in this framing.

But as I got closer, I noticed a bunch of other buildings in what we'd probably call the side yard of the house. They looked like little houses, cabins much like the ones in Heavenland, and I realized quickly that this was exactly what they were. Slave cabins. I was surprised to see them so close there. I had imagined that their houses would all be kept out of sight, that the slaves were separated from their master.

As I walked, it occurred to me—it was a long lane—that it made no sense for me to think that the slaves were kept separate. Of course they were close, at least if they worked in and for the people in the house. It would have been ridiculous for them to have to travel even the length of this driveway to get to the house. That would have taken away valuable work time.

I wondered where I had begun to think that slave houses were in separate places. I wasn't taught it since I didn't go to school, but I figured it must have been one of those things I just absorbed. An idea that came to me because of the way we talk about slavery—as an ancient and terrible thing that happened way back when and that people would have hidden, even in those days, because it was clearly so bad.

But, of course, no one thought it was bad then. In fact, we fought an *entire war* because we didn't think it was bad. We thought it was right, if not a natural order, then at least the best way of things. Ah, we made me sick.

When I reached the spot in the drive where it curved to the right toward a large set of steps, a tall, thin black man approached me. "Missus, how may I help?"

This was my cue. I took a deep breath. "I'm here to see Mr. Poke about some people."

Shelby had warned me against using the word "slaves" because people tried to be high-minded about owning other people and so called them simply "servants" or "my people." I tried to sound casual. "I need to make a purchase."

"The master is out presently," the man said, "but if you'd care to wait, we expect him shortly."

His English was very formal, clearly rehearsed. I thought immediately of Mr. Carson on *Downton Abbey*, how he had adopted the formal ways of the house as part of his position. Then, I thought of what Jed had told me his teacher said about a character named Uncle Tom, and I felt horrible. As far as I was concerned, Uncle Tom got a bad rap; he did what he needed to do to survive, and I gave him a million points for perseverance.

"Yes, that would be fine."

"Right this way, ma'am." The gentleman led me to the front porch of the house and left me to settle into a very comfortable chair overlooking the farmyard. In the movies and photographs I'd seen of plantations, the view overlooked a vista, perhaps with mountains in the distance. In the foreground, a lawn that would have made the most skilled soccer player envious stretched for the length of several football fields. It was idyllic, this scene, so perfect it almost hurt.

But now, here, the scene was very different. Oh, the porch was grand, and the mountains were there, but there was no lawn. Just beyond a short—maybe fifteen square foot—lawn, there was a fence, and beyond it, sheep were grazing. Just beyond that, the crops were planted. Tobacco, it looked like. Maybe. I wasn't really up to speed on my crops.

All through the rows of plants, I could see people bent and working. Some of the people were so small that they had to be children. Dozens of people out there, backs bent with the sun shining down on them. Just now, the air was cool, but I could already taste August coming. And August in Virginia is no joke.

No wonder Poke had time to snoop and make other people's lives miserable. He had a whole workforce doing his farm labor for him, and he didn't even have to pay them.

My stomach began to ache something fierce. This was so disgusting.

But I knew I needed to stay in character, even though it seemed like I was alone. I'd seen a couple of pairs of eyes peek up over the porch, and I knew that as quiet as the slave quarter looked to my left, the people there were watching me. I'd be watching a stranger come onto my place too.

To seem settled and comfortable and to keep myself from sprinting to the quarter and saying, "Hurry. Run. Head north," I imagined what all an adult could get done in a day if they never had to do a thing for themselves. Since I'd never worked a day in my life, I thought of Mrs. Wilson. She was a school teacher, so she left early in the mornings and came home just after Jed in the afternoons. Then, she graded papers and prepped for the next day after supper. In addition to that, she cooked all the family's meals; Mr. Wilson chipped in from time to time, but cooking wasn't really his forte. She managed the family's finances. She took care of making sure Jed had clothes and all the things he needed for school and so much more.

Then, I imagined what all she could get done if she had someone to do all those things for her. She'd go in and teach the class, sure, but then, her slaves would prep the lessons and grade the papers. Other people would cook her family's meals and be sure Jed had everything he needed. They'd tend her flower gardens and wash her clothes. They'd even get her clothes out and put her in them if she wanted. With all that extra time, she'd be able to start that cut flower business she'd dreamed of for the farm, and she'd have the free labor to make it successful right from the start. Oh, the things she could get done if she had someone else do everything for her.

Suddenly, slave labor made sense—not morally, of course—but if you had to go from having everything done for you to doing it all yourself or having to pay someone to do it, you'd fight hard to stop that from happening. I finally got why all those people fought the civil war. It wasn't about principal; it was about greed.

Slavery was wrong, horribly wrong, but I could see why white plantation owners had fought hard to not only keep slavery but to keep their slaves uneducated and isolated. Add to that the fact that black people made up a good portion of Poke's wealth, and he had a very vested interest in keeping them enslaved to him. My stomach started to ache again.

After about an hour, I began to wonder if Poke was going to show and had just made up my mind to tell the butler that I'd seek Poke another time when a carriage pulled up the lane. Two black men jumped off the back and opened the doors of the carriage so that Poke and a young woman could step out.

He kissed her on the cheek, and she went around the side of the house as the butler spoke directly into Poke's ear. I saw Poke's eyes train toward me and a slight smile cross his face. Now, my stomach really hurt.

Elias Poke was a man of average height with very pale skin and bright-red hair. He walked with a slight lean backwards, as if he were always trying to get a good look at things before he reached them. He also had absolutely horrible teeth. I could see that from the porch.

I stood as calmly as I could and waited for him to come to me. When he arrived a few moments later, he had a pipe smoking in his lips, and a young black girl was carrying a tray with iced tea to a small table on the porch. "My man didn't tell me your name," he said as he gestured for me to sit.

"That would be, sir, because I did not share it with him. I'm Mrs. Courtney Wallace from Washersburg, Maryland. I'm staying with cousins over toward Somerset and thought I'd take the opportunity to visit and inquire while I was free."

"My man said you walked here. That's quite a walk from Orange, several miles at least."

My throat tightened. "Oh, yes, I did. But just from the end of the lane. My cousins dropped me off on the way to Gordonsville to do a bit of shopping. I told them I'd enjoy the walk and that I'd see them on their way back."

Something in his shoulders loosened then. "I'll look forward to meeting the. . . What did you say their name was?"

"I didn't, sir." I could hardly breathe, but then I remembered that families were few but spread wide here. "The Madisons, sir."

The shock was very brief but still there, a flash in his eyes. I had just hinted to Poke that I was related to the former president of the United States, James Madison. Now, I had to hope he didn't know them.

"Oh, yes. Fine family. I look forward to meeting them when they come back for you later."

I took a long but hopefully lady-like sip of tea and then sat back in my chair, my gloved hands folded in my lap. "I'm afraid that introductions will have to come at another time. They were heading on to Washington for a visit. Their, um, boy Marcus will be by to get me shortly." One of the young men from the village was coming by wagon to pick me up because it would be strange for a woman to walk home at the end of the day. Strange enough for her to have walked in.

"Oh, that's too bad. Another time then." He took a puff of his pipe. "Ben mentioned you were here about some people." His relaxed posture felt a little too practiced to me.

I sat back a bit in my chair. "Yes, sir. In particular, I'm looking for a little girl to be a companion to my daughter, Samantha. My brother oversees things for us, but since my husband passed away, it's just me and Sam, and I know she'd like a companion, a girl we could raise up to be a house girl." I was speaking entirely out of what I'd seen of movies and read in books, and I sure hoped I wasn't flubbing this up big time.

"All right. Just the girl then?" Poke was still leaning back in his hair, his left leg crossed over his right knee.

"Perhaps. But I do have a bit of money to spend on people, field hands and perhaps a washerwoman, if you have good, er, stock to recommend. My husband left me a sum for this purpose, and while some might explore many avenues, I prefer to get all my people at one time simply for the ease of it."

That flicker of a smile crossed Poke's face again. "I completely understand. If you don't mind, let me step inside and check my books." He stood.

I rose with him, and this made him frown. "No need. Please sit. I'll be back shortly."

In any twenty-first-century movie or TV show, this is where the spy would ask to use the facilities, but I had no idea how that might work here ("Do you have a guest chamber pot I could use?"), so I sat back down as gently as I could and watched him walk off the porch.

As soon as he was through the door, I jumped up and crept to the nearby window on my hands and knees. I could only hope those little eyes weren't peering over the edge of the porch then.

I peeked in and saw Poke right there on the other side of the glass. I flattened myself against the boards of the porch floor.

A few seconds later, I braved another peek and saw him close a green book and put it in the center drawer of the desk just to the right of the window.

Then, I hauled myself up, dusted off my knees, and sat down just as Poke returned to the porch.

"I do believe I can help, Mrs. Wallace. But, of course, it'll take me a bit of time to gather the people for you to evaluate. Shall we meet back here in two days' time?"

I had no idea what to say, so I nodded.

A long moment of silence came down over the porch. As I took a look around the farm, I saw lots of little buildings—not just the slave cabins—and lots of people moving between them, quick and efficient like a city. A young white boy—a little older than Jed, I thought—was leaning against one of the buildings and staring at me. I felt very self-conscious. Maybe he's onto me. But as soon as I had the thought, he took a step back and went on around the building.

As my wait grew even longer, I began to worry over what kind of small talk I was going to make with a slave trader when I saw Marcus from the village coming up the lane in the wagon.

"That's my ride," I said as I stood.

Poke gave me a strange look.

"I mean, Marcus has come at my cousin's behest to fetch me. I best be going. Thank you for your time."

"Thank you, Mrs. Wallace. We'll be seeing you again real soon." His voice was icy, and my body turned cold. He knew.

Then, he took a step forward, and I put out my hand, grateful for Sharon's training about how a man in this time needed a quiet permission to touch a woman. He bent and kissed my hand, leaving his lips on my skin just a bit too long. Then, he stood up and smiled. It would have been a creepy grin in any case, but with those yellowing, rotten teeth, it was especially awful.

Marcus had pulled the wagon to the back of the house, so I went down the front steps and stood there waiting. I could see Poke on the porch above and behind me, but he was far enough away to not hear a tiny voice say, "Missus, you need that book?"

I turned around and acted as if I was adjusting my skirt. I saw a slip of a boy there in the azaleas. His skin was the color of walnut bark, and he looked like he hadn't eaten in days.

Poke couldn't know I was talking to one of his people. I turned my body away from him, so he couldn't see my mouth. "Who are you, handsome?"

I heard the boy shuffle his feet. "I'm Cato. I can get you that book for LaKeemba, missus."

I was a bit surprised he knew LaKeemba, but then, what didn't surprise me? "Cato, that is very brave of you, but it's okay. We'll get it."

"No, you won't, missus. Master knows who you is. You need me."

I had no idea how this tiny child knew what Poke knew, but if he knew the folks from Heavenland, I figured he was probably a good read on people.

"Cato, it's too dangerous." I was nervous for the boy just talking to him like this.

"Not as dangerous as you not having it. I'll bring it to the village tonight, before Master and his men come."

I almost turned around then. "Before they come?" I heard the anxiousness in my voice.

"Yes, missus. He know who you are, and he coming tonight. I'll beat him there."

I didn't like this. I didn't like it at all. If Poke was coming already, then we couldn't waste time.

"You bring the book and anything else you can carry, Cato, all right? You won't be coming back, you understand?"

"Yes, missus. Me and Squeak will be there soon as the sun down good."

"Squeak?"

"My sister. She one and can't quite talk yet. I'll carry her."

I had a horrible vision of this tiny boy carrying his even tinier sister through the dark woods. What if they got caught? "Cato, are you sure?" My voice was pointed like a dart.

"Yes, missus."

"All right. You know the way?"

"Yes, missus. Been there plenty of times to see my mama."

Just then, Marcus came around the house with the wagon, and Cato slipped back into the bushes. My heart was in my throat.

14

*W*hen I got back to the village, I leapt—okay, I lumbered—off the cart and waddled as fast as I could over to LaKeemba's cabin. I was talking before I even got through the door. "Cato. . . little boy. . . stealing ledger. . . coming here."

"Sit, Mavis. Sit." Shelby pulled one of the cushions over and handed me a glass of water. "Now, what about Cato?" She was leaning forward, looking me close in the face.

I gulped it down, took a deep breath, and told them about Cato and Squeak, about the book. "I didn't know what to do. He seemed so sure, and we had to whisper, and I knew that Poke—"

"Breathe, Mavis." LaKeemba put a hand on the back of my neck, and I instantly felt calmer. "Cato and Squeak will be fine. They come here a lot. You've probably even seen them." She glanced at Shelby, who was smiling by the door. "Shelby's their mother."

My eyes went very wide, and I stood up. "What? I didn't know you had kids."

"You never asked," Shelby said with a sad smile.

I sat down hard. "You're right. I'm sorry. And Poke, um, owns them?"

"So to speak. Not sure I believe anybody can own anybody else, but yes, he holds their papers."

I nodded, but I was confused. "He holds Mercy's papers, too, right?" I gestured to the four-year-old asleep on a mattress at the back of the cabin.

"He does," LaKeemba said, "but I've never tried to run." She cut her eyes at Shelby and smiled.

"You tried to run?" I was feeling somewhere between proud and terrified for Shelby.

"Yes, ma'am, I did, and I would have made it, too, if Squeak hadn't gotten sick. She was coughing, and the catchers heard us."

The slave catchers. My heart sank. "You had to come back." Tears pooled in my eyes.

"I did, and Poke knew that I'd never leave without my babies. So, he kept them. Told me if I ever tried to take them again, he'd kill them. Told Cato the same thing about me." Her voice had gone icy, and she was gritting her teeth.

"Don't you just want to kill him?" My heart was beating in my ears, and I had to force my fingers out of fists.

"Every day." Shelby took a deep breath. "But here's the thing, if I did that, they'd actually own my kids, right? They'd be able to sell them off, or worse. So, I keep my cool and plan."

"Exactly," LaKeemba said from the doorway. "I take it Poke is onto you."

"Oh yes, I definitely think so. At least he seemed suspicious at the end of our conversation." I was finally catching my breath, and the adrenaline of the outing was wearing off. I could have put my head down and gone to sleep right there.

"Good. Good," LaKeemba said as she walked out the door. "Let's go tell everyone."

I gave a long sigh and stood up. But my weariness didn't last long because when I walked out of the cabin, Jed nearly tackled me. "Where have you been?" His face was flushed, and it was only then that I realized he must have come back to find me gone.

"Oh, Jed, I'm sorry. I had an errand to run."

"In that?" He gave my dress a once over, and then his smile turned into a doubled-over belly laugh.

I wanted to be offended, but I couldn't help but laugh with him. I knew I looked ridiculous.

"We need you two over here," LaKeemba called.

Jed and I looked at each other, kept giggling, and walked over to the fire. It's awfully hard for me to be lady-like anytime, but ironically, wearing a big ole dress made it even harder, so I tucked the dress between my legs and dropped to the log with all the grace of a bag of flour.

The sight of my gracelessness caused a titter around the fire, and soon, everyone was laughing—some people so hard that they had tears streaming down their faces. Before you knew it, we were in one of those great spots where everyone laughs and then settles themselves until someone gets going again, and soon the whole group is laughing. I heard someone across the circle snort, and I farted so loudly that Jed couldn't breathe from laughter. Even LaKeemba was bent over and holding her stomach. It was glorious.

Finally, the laughter settled into the kind of quiet that comes to a group of people when they feel totally safe with each other. It felt amazing, even though I knew we were all still uneasy. Still, scared with company is way better than scared alone.

After a few minutes, LaKeemba had me tell the story about my visit to Poke's place, how he planned to come over tonight, and how we might not need to go toward his place at all because the records might come to us.

"He'll be coming to check on us, for certain now," Sharon said. "He knows we're up to something. And he'll be trying to figure what."

A murmur went around the fire, and a shiver ran up my spine.

"We need to prepare. You know what to do." LaKeemba stood and walked toward her cabin.

I hadn't mentioned Cato and Squeak because it didn't feel necessary, and Shelby thanked me. "No one needs to be worrying about those babies besides you and me."

I smiled and gave her a quick hug.

"Plus, you know we love everybody here, but loving people and trusting they always make good choices aren't the same thing," Shelby said.

"Preach," Sharon said as she walked over. "Most of us is wise folks, but you never know if somebody might go back to Poke, thinking they'd be doing little Cato a favor." She winked at me then. "Come on, Mavis. Let's get you out of that get-up and back into your blue jeans."

"Thank God," I said and gave Jed's arm a quick squeeze as I headed back to LaKeemba's cabin.

We spent the rest of the afternoon preparing, packing but in such a way that it didn't look like we were packing. Most people here were filling feed sacks and handkerchiefs, so we didn't have to do anything as obvious as keep suitcases hidden. But we did have to be sure quilts stayed on mattresses and clothes were kept on hooks by doors. The fire was tended solid so that it seemed obvious we were planning to stay around a while.

But behind the scenes, pillowcases were filled with precious things: photographs smuggled through time and tiny dolls whittled from branches by the fireside. Jed made sure all our things were gathered, although we didn't have much, so there was no need for a big bag. Pockets would do.

After the physical things were tended, the Heavenland folks set about making sure the magic was good. Shelby refortified the net, and I finally got a hint of Alonso's gift at work. He moved from person to person, putting a hand to the skin of everyone there. When he came to me, I felt a jolt, like I'd touched a blanket on a dry day. "You'll have it when you need it," was all he said as he moved on to the next person.

Just after nightfall, Cato and Squeak arrived. Squeak was getting an eerily silent piggyback ride as they came into camp. As soon as I saw them, relief flooded my body.

Cato had a satchel tied around his waist, and I could see flashes of a green book cover pressed against his belly, where he had tucked the ledger into the waistband of his pants.

My relief didn't last long. As soon as Cato got close enough, he shout-whispered, "They're coming. I don't think they saw us leave, but they've got wagons and horses. A whole lot of men."

Shelby hugged her children and told them to go with Lizzie. We'd fortified what Sharon had told me was a brush arbor behind the village. Normally, it was where the Christians among the villagers would go to church on the Sundays they were there. A small square of poles and sturdy trees was overlaid with branches and leaves to make a dry space for people to gather. We put up make-shift walls of brush around it—not too noticeable but enough to hide the children from view. Two men were guarding that space, but they had handsaws to make it look like they were gathering firewood. We knew our best defense was to have everything look normal.

It didn't take long for Poke and his posse to show up. They rode into town, and while they didn't hoot and holler like teenage boys on their way to a big football game, their faces showed the glee of those who thought they'd be easily victorious. As soon as I saw them, I shoved Jed behind me.

They came with machetes and muskets, hoes and pitchforks, and I couldn't help but think of all those lynch mobs I'd seen pictures of. It was terrifying.

Jed, of course, had stepped out from behind me right away. As we stood near the fire, both of us trying to act surprised that they had come and nonchalant about their visit, Poke walked up and said, "Thought I wouldn't recognize you, huh?"

I took a deep breath. "Whatever do you mean?" Somehow, the only old-fashioned way of speech I knew was from *Gone with the Wind*. "We had never met until today."

LaKeemba had suggested we play ignorant of Poke's people as much as possible. She figured Poke would know we were lying, but it might give him pause.

I glanced over at Sharon, who was just behind Poke on the other side of the fire, and she gave me an almost imperceptible nod. *Keep him talking.*

Poke laughed. "Don't play dumb with me. I know who you are, Mavis, er—" he fumbled here, searching for a surname I didn't have. "You were in New York just a few days ago, Paris before that, and several other places and times, too, I do believe."

I tried to act the right amount of shocked as I saw the villagers moving about the gathering of cabins as if they were about regular business when really, they were getting ready.

"I don't know what you mean, Mr. Poke." I think I even batted my eyelashes a little.

"What's a white woman and boy doing here anyway? Why would you want to hang out with a bunch of—"

Before Poke could finish, Jed jumped in front of me. "Don't you call them that."

Poke laughed again, but I could also see a bit of surprise. He wasn't used to being confronted.

"Don't like that word, boy? Does it offend your sensibilities, nig—?"

I pushed Jed to the side again. "That's enough, Mr. Poke. I know here that language is commonplace, but where we come from, we don't use that word. It's ugly, and the hearts of the people who say it are uglier."

I thought maybe I'd gone too far then, but I saw Sharon give me a wink as she walked slowly around the fire as if she was just coming to support me.

The ire was up in Poke then, though. His face had gotten all blotchy, and I thought he might hit me. In fact, I'm pretty sure his hand was raised when a tiny woman I'd only seen in passing reached up from where she was crouching over a stewpot on the fire and laid her hands upon Poke's arm.

He screamed and then fell over, almost into the fire.

I barely had time to hear Jed yell, "Yes. It's on," before the magic broke loose.

Sharon dropped another of the men. Shelby blew a cloud of powder in the faces of the men on one wagon, and they dropped instantly to sleep. Another man lit the other wagon on fire with a snap of his fingers and pushed it out and away from the building as the white men jumped off it and ran into the woods.

Alonso moved calmly from man to man, acting like he was going to grab their weapons, but instead sending what I can only presume was a hard, electrifying jolt through the metal and dropping them like hot potatoes. Another woman, who I'd seen regularly sewing in a corner, stepped forward, swept the legs out of two men with one of her own, and then stood with a foot on each of their throats until Sharon could come over and put them to sleep. Most impressive was a thin reed of a man who conjured the grapevines above to swing down and grab up two of the men by their ankles. If it hadn't been so scary, it would have made a great show.

It was all over in a matter of moments. All the white men were either asleep, were dangling above our heads, or had run away. Only Poke was there, wide awake and writhing. He eked out a "You'll pay—" but Sharon took a step toward him, and he stopped talking immediately.

LaKeemba came over from where she'd been watching from her cabin. "Mr. Poke, we're going to be leaving now. As you can see, it's best if you don't follow us or try to find us."

Poke tried to sit up then. "You know you can't do that."

"Oh, yes, we can." She held up the ledger, and dozens of slips of papers slid from it into the fire before LaKeemba dropped the book into the flames and breathed on them until they were roaring.

I thought Poke might have an aneurysm right there. "You'll pay for this."

I expected Jed to say, "What a cliché. Can't you come up with something better than that?" Jed hated the one-liners that movie villains threw out. But when he didn't speak, I looked over to him. He was gone.

My eyes scanned the village. Nothing. I ran to the brush arbor. Not there either.

Then, I heard it. My name. Shouted from far out in the forest. "Mavis! Help!"

JEDIDIAH

I don't know how we missed him, but he had me around the throat with a hand over my mouth faster than I could speak, and he was strong. He dragged me into the woods so quick I couldn't even get my feet under me.

I could feel that evil out here, and with every minute, it got closer, almost like it was feeding on my fear.

When I finally got a look at the man's face, I saw he was just a teenage boy, a few years older than me, but not really a man yet. But he was stronger than me by ten-fold. Bike riding is great for leg strength, but suddenly I wished I'd used Dad's weight set out in the barn more.

Still, I fought as hard as I could. I kicked out my arms and legs and tried to dig my heels into the ground, but he just kept me tight against his chest and dragged me on.

At one point, I finally wrenched my head free and screamed for Mavis, but I was sure we were too far out. She'd never hear me.

I knew then that it was on me, and that gave me strength. I kicked the boy hard in the shin and took a step to run as hard as I could, but I froze in mid-sprint.

The boy stepped in front of me. "I'm not going to hurt you. I just need some answers." He had his hand held out in front of him like he was going to blast me with ice, like Storm from the X-Men *or something, so I stopped fighting. He dropped his hands as he released me.*

"You're magic." I said it as matter-of-fact as if I'd said, "You have red hair," which he did.

"Don't know what you call it, but yeah, I can do that." He pointed to my body.

I wanted to be mad. I wanted to scream and yell until the villagers came and rescued me, but I didn't. "Does Poke know?"

"No way. I'm not telling my dad about this. I see what he says about you frea—about you people."

I let out a long sigh and sat down right there in the middle of the woods.

"You know they're going to come after you, right?" I asked him.

"Yep."

"You're not scared."

"Nope."

"Think you should be?"

"Nope. I figure you won't let them hurt me seeing as how we're the same and all."

He was right, but I wasn't about to let him know that. Truth was, I didn't want anybody to get hurt, even Poke. I looked closer at the boy then. "You been watching me?"

"All of you."

I took a deep breath. I could see it there on him: the loneliness, the sadness, the fear. I could see it, and I recognized it because I'd lived it. I didn't trust him, but I understood him. "Okay, tell me about this thing you can do."

The boy gave me a long look, then dropped his shoulders and let out a sigh. "I can stop stuff. Raindrops. Bugs. A pot of stew boiling. Just always been able to do it, but a few days ago, I got stronger. That's about when I heard Daddy talking about you and that woman. Figured it had something to do with you all being here."

I had no idea what Mavis and I had to do with his powers getting stronger, but now wasn't really the time to figure that out, so I nodded. "Okay, then, so we've got to help each other, I suppose." I dropped my head into my hands to think a minute and decided. "We're about to run. Want to come?" Some part of me thought this was a really bad idea, but more of me could see this guy was hurting and needed help.

"Already packed." The boy pointed to a knapsack behind a tree.

"Well, let's go then, um. . ."

"Charlie."

I put out my hand like Dad had taught me, and he shook it. "I'm Jed. Let's go."

15

$\mathcal{W}$e found Jed almost immediately since they were coming our way. But I wasn't very happy to see him with the red-headed kid I'd seen at Poke's place, and I was even less happy when I learned he was Poke's son.

I had a whole what-were-you-thinking speech planned and was just leaning back to get a good breath, when Jed said, "Show them." His voice was soft and gentle, and he was looking right at that kid.

We'd just come back into the village, and everyone was there; pillowcases and burlaps sacks were waiting by cabin doors. I should have figured something was up when everyone stopped and looked up even before they were able to see Jed and Charlie coming up behind me.

Then, Charlie raised his right hand with his palm out and his fingers tilted to the right. He directed it toward the fire, and I saw him take a deep breath. I was waiting for something to happen, watching his face for some change, when I noticed the light was different. It was steady, like light from a lamp.

I turned slowly and saw that the fire was completely still. It looked like fire—all the golds and reds and even the cold blues by the coals—but nothing was moving. It was just as still as a photograph.

I looked from the fire to Charlie and back again. Then, he let out a long sigh and lowered his hand. The light began to dance again, and when I glanced back to the fire, it was just like it had always been.

LaKeemba was at the door of her cabin, and I sort of expected her to give the "back to packing" signal by waving her hand in a circle over her head. Instead, she was stock-still, almost as if Charlie had stopped her too.

I looked from her to Alonso and then on to Shelby. All of them were staring at Charlie as if they had just seen a ghost. (Briefly, I wondered if any of them had the ability to see ghosts. But then, I figured that would be a very Mavis thing to ask at that moment, so I kept my mouth shut.)

Jed looked just as puzzled as I felt, so I inched over to him. "What's going on?"

"I have no idea." He looked at Charlie.

Charlie shrugged. "You think I know what's up? I'm new at this, remember."

The sound of Charlie's voice—still a little squeaky from the voice change that hadn't even hit Jed yet—got everyone moving. But there were a lot of glances flying around there as if everyone else was having a conversation I wasn't in on.

"We are ready." LaKeemba made the announcement with finality and began to lead a long procession toward the pin oak.

I kept Jed and Charlie ahead of me, and I heard Jed lean over to Charlie and say, "You're sure? I don't think you can come back after this."

Charlie didn't even look around. Just nodded as he kept his eyes on the tree.

Soon, we had formed a circle around the oak, and LaKeemba said, "The Wilson farm, the day Jed and Mavis came," and began to lead the procession around the tree, one by one. I didn't know how this was going to go, all of us suddenly walking out of the woods. It seemed unlikely that Sharon could explain a few dozen people appearing from nowhere, but it made sense to go there. Poke's men didn't—as best as we could tell—know where or when Jed and I were from. So, when Shelby had suggested the farm, I couldn't come up with a reason to say it was bad except that it was "going to look weird." Magic people don't really have a great aversion to looking weird, I guess, because they had basically ignored me.

Slowly, the line moved forward and disappeared, and soon, it was our turn. Jed took a picture out of his back pocket. Over his shoulder, I could see it was a photo of the farm taken from just about the spot where we would come out of the forest. He handed it to Charlie. "Think of here."

Charlie stared at the picture and then nodded. Jed went first. Then Charlie. Then me.

For the two seconds it took to make the transition, I was terrified.

Then, I stepped around the tree into the brighter forest of our time, and there was everyone, even Charlie, waiting for the rest of us to follow. Once everyone had come through, we walked out of the woods together, and I couldn't help but imagine we looked like either an invading army or a bunch of quasi-hippies bent on taking over the farm for our commune.

Sharon was beside LaKeemba, and as soon as Mr. Wilson stepped out of his shop at the back of the barn, Sharon started talking to him. I couldn't hear most of what she said, something about "research project," "farm life," and "educational opportunity," but Mr. Wilson didn't seem flummoxed at all after the first few moments. By the time Jed reached his dad to hug him, there was talk of putting yurts up by the tree line, mowing the hayfield to make for more comfortable sleeping, and dinner by the firepit.

As everyone else wandered off to get camp set up, Jed stood close to his dad, tucked into his arm. "Son, this is great," Mr. Wilson was beaming. "I love that you've gotten so interested in agriculture." Then his brow furrowed a bit. "I'm not sure how to ask this though; I don't want to sound racist."

I could almost guess what he was going to say, and I'd have asked the question too.

"Why are you three the only white people?"

Jed looked at me and then at Charlie. "I think the right question to ask, Dad, would be, why haven't I been one of the few white people in a group before?"

Whew, that kid was smart. Smarter than me, that was for sure.

Mr. Wilson looked a little chagrined, but he nodded. "Good point, son. Good point." He gave Jed a quick side hug. "Now, are you going to introduce me to your friends? Let's start with the two of you. I'm Leon." He extended his hand to me.

I was almost too surprised to take it. I'd never, not once, heard him call himself by his first name. I knew it, of course. I'd seen it on mail and heard Mrs. Wilson call him that. But for him to tell me his name was Leon. . . My mind was blown. It took me a long second before I grabbed his hand and said, "I'm Mavis."

Mr. Wil—I mean, Leon shot a glance to Jed, and I realized my mistake instantly. But Jed covered for me. "Crazy, huh? She's from just up the road, so maybe I heard her name and called my imaginary friend that."

"You had an imaginary friend?" I was grinning.

"Oh, this kid. Mavis was his best friend. He wouldn't go anywhere without her coming along. She always gave him good advice too. One time, she told Jed that he should try building, and soon, he had cleaned up every twig in the yard and created an entire castle. Remember that was your 'I want to be a knight stage.'" He looked at his son, who blushed as red as Charlie's hair.

"That was good advice. Good for him and good for us." He let out a short sigh. "I'm kind of sad she's not around anymore."

Jed looked like he wished he'd told the truth—all watery-eyed and frowny-faced—but I gave him a gentle poke to the belly. "Oh, don't be embarrassed, kid. A lot of us have friends no one else can see." I tried to make my voice light, but I was working really hard to force back tears myself.

Mr. Wilson looked to my left and put out his hand again. "And you are?"

"Charlie. Charlie Poke, sir. Nice to meet you."

"Nice to meet you, too, Charlie." He grabbed Charlie around the shoulders with his other arm, and I saw Charlie stiffen a bit. I wondered if his dad had been that sweet to him. From the look on his face, I doubted it. "Let's go meet everyone else."

Soon, all the introductions had been made, and Mrs. Wilson had come home from work with two giant hams. Jed had texted her to let her know we had company and if she could please pick up food for another sixty or so people. As usual, she hadn't been fazed at all. She was my role model.

Someone had built a big spit over the firepit, and they slid those hams onto two pieces of rebar that Mr. Wilson dug out of the barn and washed up. Within minutes, the entire farmyard smelled amazing. Jed and Charlie pulled some folding tables out of the hayloft, and Alonso and a couple of the women joined Mrs. Wilson in the farmhouse kitchen to make potato salad and biscuits.

I snuck off to the side a bit and watched. Partly out of habit. Partly out of fatigue. I wasn't used to talking to this many people in a day. What I saw delighted me: hospitality at its finest and good guests. No one expected the Wilsons to do everything for them, but the Wilsons also wanted to show their guests courtesy and respect. It felt like the Wilson family had just gotten a whole lot bigger, and I liked it.

Jed threw blankets on the grass around the fire, and I grabbed a few camp chairs from the old horse stalls in the barn. Then, everyone sat and ate, passing dishes and serving one another with the big spoons and forks stuck into each bowl.

I ate well, and soon, I was so tired I almost fell asleep sitting there, the warmth from the flames making me relax for the first time in days. The villagers were telling stories about their adventures—always truthful but also always presented with that kind of language that felt like legend rather than experience. Lots of "You wouldn't believe," and, "Lo and behold." No need to get the Wilsons worried about their son's new friends.

Slowly, people began to wander to the tents they'd staked earlier, and I saw Jed look longingly at the window into his room. Only then did I wonder where I was going to sleep. I figured Charlie was going to bunk up with Jed, but I sure wasn't going to take my butt into Jed's room now.

I began to think I was going to end up in the hayloft again since I didn't have a tent to myself when Alonso came over. "We've got your space ready, Mavis."

I looked up at him, saw him looking right at me, and I felt like I might cry again. "What?"

"You can't be sleeping in the hayloft, woman, and those hips of yours will not tolerate the ground."

I looked down at my hips and gave them a little shimmy. Humor was always the best way to deal with overwhelming emotion, at least for me.

"Come with me." He led me to a large tent pitched right next to LaKeemba's. It reminded me of those tents in those movies depicting Morocco. A camping lamp hung from a hook in the middle of the space, and on one side was a cot and a wool blanket. To the other side, someone had fashioned a clothes' rack out of branches, and on it were three sets of clothes—leggings, a couple pairs of jeans, and the flowing blouses I loved to wear—and below those, a pair of sneakers and a pair of sandals.

Then, I began to cry in earnest. They had realized I had nowhere to sleep and nothing else to wear, and they had gotten me what I needed without me even asking. I had never been so seen.

Alonso directed me to the soft, flannel PJs draped on the bed, gave me a hug, and shut the tent flap behind him.

I fell asleep instantly, and it was blissful. I felt loved and wanted, and my dreams were light and beautiful—all butterflies and apple cobbler—my favorites.

Sometime in the night, when it was darkest, someone stepped into my tent. I tried to pretend I was asleep, hoping they'd just go away. Then, I felt a blade against my throat.

"Mavis," a voice hissed. "You're coming with me."

JEDIDIAH

The next morning, I'd almost forgotten all that had happened. My sheets were so soft, and the sunbeam hit my face the way it did every morning, except for those mornings when it was still dark when I had to get up. (For the record, I was not a fan.) It felt like I should be going to school, and I started to figure out if I'd done all my homework.

But then, all in a rush, I remembered. I went from feeling comfortable to feeling like a frog on a hot car hood.

I jumped up and nearly fell over Charlie, who was curled up like a roly-poly bug in a sleeping bag by my bed. He started moving when I stepped over him, and when I came back from the bathroom, he was sitting up.

I laughed, and he just stared at me. "Your hair, man. It's standing straight up." I saw his cheeks get real red and felt kind of bad.

His voice was quiet when he said, "Oh yeah, it does this every morning. Do you have a comb I can use?"

I tossed him the one on my dresser and wondered for a second if his comb looked the same as mine. Since he just pulled it through his hair without really looking at it, I figured so.

I seemed to float down the stairs, and Mom was there waiting for me with a whole plate of bacon, a big bowl of cheesy eggs, and grits with lots of butter, salt, and pepper. My favorite breakfast.

Charlie's eyes got huge when he saw all the food on the table. He looked at my dad, then me, then my mom, and then back at me. "This is all for just the four of us?"

Mom laughed. "Well, I know you guys must be hungry. You're growing after all."

"And farming is hard work," Dad added.

Charlie and I shot each other a look but then dug in. It was delicious. I ate at least six pieces of bacon and an entire cereal bowl full of grits too. When I was done, I felt like I'd swallowed an inner tube. I sat back in my chair and groaned.

Charlie did the same, and then we laughed. It was like the day before by the campfire, but without Mavis's farts. Just the thought of that got me going again. When someone knocked a few minutes later, we were all crying since we'd been laughing so hard.

Mom got up and answered the door. When she came back, her face was as stern as Principal McGeelay when I got into that spitball contest with my friend Tyler. I stopped laughing as soon as I saw her.

Sharon came in then and sat down at the table with us. She had that face that adults get that says, "The news is really bad, but I'm going to try and act like it's not." That's the worst face because it's kind of a lie but not one you can catch anybody in.

"What happened?" Charlie got the question out before I did. I guess he knew that adult face too.

"We're working on a plan, Jed, so I don't want you to worry." She was sliding the fork around on the table.

"What happened?" I asked, trying to keep the fear out of my voice.

"Alonso is gathering a team. They're probably headed out as we speak, so it's going to be okay."

"What happened?" My voice was getting louder.

"We're good at this, Jed, so you don't need to worry."

I stood up so quickly that my chair fell backwards and slammed into the tile floor. "What happened?" I yelled.

She finally looked at me then, and her face fell a little. "Mavis was kidnapped."

It felt like the floor dropped out from under my feet. "What are you talking about?"

"Last night, someone came into her tent and took her, Jed."

I had to sit down, but I couldn't move without maybe falling down. So, I just stood there.

"She's only been gone a few hours. We'll catch up to them."

"A few hours? She's been missing for a few hours, and no one knew. How is that possible? With all your magic and such, how could you not know?" I slammed my chair out of the way and headed toward Sharon.

Her voice took on a new tone then. I could feel it vibrating a little, like it was a drill moving through a piece of wood, but it wasn't wood she was burrowing into; it was my mind. "Jed, you know that we only joke about using magic because it's funny to think about a bunch of farmers who can do magic, right?"

Something felt like it moved behind my eyes then, a little click of recognition, and I nodded. Not because Sharon's word spells had worked on me (they didn't), but because I realized that Mom and Dad weren't supposed to know about their magic—our magic.

"Right," I said and saw Charlie nodding from the corner of my eye. "But seriously, how didn't anyone hear someone take her? I mean, Mavis isn't exactly quiet, right?"

"We're not sure." Sharon was speaking carefully here, but she wasn't using her power anymore. "We're still trying to figure that out."

"How can we help?" Dad was looking concerned, but in a way that told me he was just worried about my friend and also about me because I was worried about my friend. "Should we call the police?"

"We've already informed the proper authorities. Don't worry, Mr. and Mrs. Wilson. We have lots of people with lots of talents in our group. We'll track down Mavis." She stood to leave. "Do you mind if we borrow Jed and Charlie for a bit?" I could hear just a gentle vibration behind her voice. "They may be able to help us with our search since they knew Mavis pretty well."

"Sure. Just let us know if we can be of any help. Any help at all." Mom stood and began clearing dishes. "We'll be here all day." I could tell they were worried, but more like how they'd be worried if a chicken got out since it would eventually come back. I tried not to be mad at them; I knew they would have been really worried if Sharon had let them be. But I still felt a little hurt.

The three of us left just as Dad began to load the dishwasher. As soon as we were out of earshot, I said, "What is going on, Sharon? No one has special powers that lets you hear well or see in the dark? How did someone get through all of you to get Mavis? And why did they want Mavis? She's not even magical."

"We don't know, Jed." My face must have looked frustrated because she added. "We're going to figure this out. It seems likely that someone with magic came into the campsite. Maybe someone who can deaden sound."

"Or someone who can make people stay asleep." Charlie's voice was very quiet.

"Charlie, do you know something?" Sharon had stopped walking and was facing Charlie now. "If you do, it would be very helpful to know what you know."

He looked at Sharon and then down at his feet. "One of the catchers back from my place, well, he can make people sleep for as long as he wants just by whistling a tune."

"What tune is that, Charlie?"

"'Dixie,' ma'am."

"Oh, good Lord." I thought Sharon's head might pop right off her body she was so mad, but I wasn't sure why. I almost started whistling the song myself. It was catchy, and we'd sung it in fourth-grade music class. Our teacher had told us it was a tribute to the South, but Sharon seemed to think different. Now didn't seem the time to ask why though.

Nope, now was the time to find my best friend. . . And fast.

16

*W*hen someone threatens your life, you remember the voice. As soon as I heard Glass speak, I could picture him in that alley, all sinister and in need of a good hair-stylist.

He and some other big dude that kept whistling bustled me out of the tent, and I did my best to make as much noise as possible. I screamed and kicked over buckets. I slammed my body into tents until they shook. But no one stirred. It was creepy, so creepy that it made me go completely still as they walked me to the black SUV that was sitting, normal as day, in the Wilsons' driveway.

I was pushed into the backseat. From the front, Glass said, "Hello, Mavis. I'm glad it worked out for us to see each other again."

I wanted to immediately clean out my ears with battery acid. He was just so smarmy, as Jed's friend Kiki would say. I decided that, for once, I was going to keep my mouth shut, so I looked out the window and held my lips tightly closed.

As we rolled down the road toward Lexington, I thought about flinging the door open and tossing myself out. I had a hunch the giant spark-plug of a man next to me would probably catch me, but only after I'd gotten halfway out. I'd likely slam my head against the car, dislocate my shoulder, and still be kidnapped.

Plus, there was no door handle. There was that.

So, I watched the Virginia countryside roll by, first on the two-lane roads, then on the highway, and then up onto I-81 toward Roanoke. The Wilsons had come this way plenty of times for trips to the mall or birthday dinners, but I'd never been able to come along. I only knew where we were going because of the big green highway signs that said, "Roanoke, 45 miles."

Soon, we were pulling off the interstate and driving through a part of the city full of low-flung buildings made of brick and some white stone looking stuff. Some of the buildings had lots of garage doors. Occasionally, there were signs with some confusing names like, "AlluroNo," but I didn't see anything that looked like a shop or a restaurant. Even in the middle of the night, the place looked pretty deserted.

We stopped behind yet another one-story building with an almost invisible entrance. I was pushed along through the door and down a long gray carpeted hall to a little room at the back of the building. If there were a two-way mirror, I'd have thought I was in a *Law and Order*-style interrogation room. That would have almost been exciting.

But nope, just a table, a half-dozen chairs, some forgotten paper clips, and a Styrofoam cup with what looked like ancient coffee inside.

Spark Plug locked the door behind him, and there I was, completely alone in a room with nothing to do. I sat quietly for a few minutes, thinking someone would surely come back and want something from me—information maybe. But when no one came, I tried to MacGyver a lock pick from the paper clips—I learned that I was not MacGyver—not Richard Dean Anderson or that new blonde kid with the chin of a comic book superhero.

So, I sat and stared. And stared. And stared.

I started to doze off because when I don't have anything to occupy me and need to escape for a bit, I sleep. My head was down on the table, but then I heard their voices—Glass and a woman. I recognized the woman's voice from somewhere, but it was hard to tell through the walls. They must have been in one of the rooms next door.

I got up and put my ear to the wall. It didn't help. I looked at the cup of coffee, flung the coffee into the corner, and then tried the cup against the wall. Worse. I sat back down and listened real hard.

"They will come," the woman was saying. "Mavis matters. More than she knows." Her voice faded there, and I almost cursed. What about me? Why do I matter so much?

Glass was shouting. "They don't even know where we took her, and you can't tell them because they'll be onto you."

Oh, this was getting good. It was feeling more and more like a real TV show. Now we had a mole. I was almost excited—okay, not excited, but entertained at least. Although I was still bothered by the fact that I knew that voice.

"We don't have to tell them. That kid can find her, no problem. He just needs a little prompting to know he can," the woman said.

"So, get prompting!" Glass sounded angry. The slamming door confirmed that.

Then, I heard the woman speak again, and I gathered she was on the phone. "Yeah, it's me. Shelby. Yeah, we have her. Yeah, she's secure. Okay, I'll wait for your instructions."

My heart was racing now, and tears welled up in my eyes. I thought of her giving me a manicure, and of the hug we shared when I said her children were coming back to her.

My friend—the woman I had thought was my friend—was a traitor. She was working with Poke. I had to warn them. I had to warn Jed.

I spent about thirty minutes walking around that room like a caged tiger. Banging on the door. Pounding on the walls to see if I could punch through them. Wishing that two-way mirror really was there so I could break it. But eventually, I realized I was not getting out of that room.

Then, I spent another few minutes crying and sulking.

Eventually, though, I decided a pity party wasn't going to do Jed or my friends any good.

So, I sat down and started to think. I thought about all the villagers and their powers. I remembered what Jed had told me about Sharon healing him with a song. I thought about the way Alonso had charged us all with. . . Well, I still wasn't sure what. Jed could see things. LaKeemba had some power of leadership. The fire starter. Charlie and his ability to stop things from moving. That dude who could make plants do what he wanted.

My friends were impressive, and every person in that village had some sort of ability. Everyone but me. Now that I wasn't imaginary—and thus, not invisible—anymore, I didn't have any skills at all, except to get kidnapped as bait.

I started to slide back into self-pity again, but then my brain snagged on something—I had been invisible once.

I took a few deep breaths like Shelby, the traitor, had taught me, and I remembered what it was like to watch TV with the Wilsons when only Jed could see me. I pictured the empty space around me, and I felt something shift, like a thin piece of fabric was draped over my head. I hadn't missed that feeling until now, but it was back, and I knew it. I was invisible.

Now, to plan.

When formulating an escape attempt, it's useful to have watched a lot of episodes of shows like *Criminal Minds*. I knew that my best hope was a sneak attack, although that sounded like something a four-year-old or a sniper would do. I wasn't exactly sneaky, but I could wallop someone good given the chance. I was confident that I could lay someone out, although I had not yet had cause to test this theory.

I thought about trying to act like I was really sick, but that felt too obvious. So instead, I tried the time-honored, "I have to use the bathroom," ruse. (It had not gone unnoticed by me that my go-to trick was the need to pee—first at Poke's and now here—but given that I did need to pee quite often, it seemed reasonable.)

Apparently, it was believable, too, because after only a minute or so of calling out as loudly and as dragged out as I could, "I need to pee. I need to *pee. I need to pee!*" I heard footsteps in the hallway and took up my position behind the door. A tiny woman opened it, and I thought I had it made—until I saw the pistol at her hip and her hand at the ready.

I hesitated for a second, and when she swung to look behind the door, I thought I was caught. However, she whipped back around and scanned the room again. Then, she was out the door and down the hall, gun drawn, shouting, "She's escaped!"

Now, I had a choice to make. I could take my chances and make my way down the hall to the front door. But then, I risked bumping into someone. I wasn't exactly a small woman, you might say, and I didn't know how gracefully I could get out of the way if someone came at me fast.

So, I opted to stay in the room. It felt like the counter-intuitive choice that would be my saving grace—sort of like hiding in plain sight, except for the sight part.

A dozen or so people ran past the door. A few peeked their heads into the room where I sat as if they might have just missed me before, all two hundred pounds of me in a ten-by-twelve space. Eventually, the hubbub died down, and the building got very quiet. Again, I was faced with a choice.

I knew I couldn't sit there forever, so as quietly as I could, I crept my way down the hall by mostly sidestepping with my back against the wall just in case. At each doorway, I waited a minute just to be sure no one would step out and slam into me as I crossed by it, and then I'd rush across.

Eventually, I made it to the front door, the breaking point of this mission. In my head, this was Operation Break-Loose, and I was the head agent. I had to open the door, which of course, was tricky. We've all seen those movies and cartoons where the invisible character gets caught because they move something that other people can see. That Millard character in those *Peculiar Children* books that Jed loved came to mind. Fortunately, my invisibility included my clothes. And always had, in case you're wondering.

But a door was another story. I knew that if anyone were watching the building, they'd see the door open, and I'd likely be caught. But if I revealed myself and they were watching, they'd have more time to see me. I decided to stay invisible and opened the door just enough to squeeze myself out.

Then, I took off. By which I mean I ran as fast as I could, which was really about the rate of a sloth after a couple of Red Bulls. Quicker than usual but still not quick. Fortunately, I was able to move from building to building and stay mostly hidden. Once I was a couple of buildings away, I slipped into another office complex, stepped into a bathroom stall, and locked the door.

I stayed there for a while, catching my breath, planning my next move, and, yes, also taking a pee.

Eventually, I let my invisibility slide off (it took me only a second to figure out how to do that), walked out of the bathroom, past the receptionist on his cellphone, and out into the street.

Now, how would I get back to the farm?

17

I made my way out of the industrial park and started heading in the direction of most of the traffic. Fortunately, Roanoke is a city that likes sidewalks, so I didn't look too out of place walking.

Eventually, I found myself in the heart of the city. Taller buildings lined the streets, and more people were moving about. It was a Wednesday, early morning by the light of it, and people wearing suits and carrying giant cups of coffee were moving at a brisk pace past the storefronts.

For the first time in my life, I realized I didn't have any money. Not that I knew anything at all what it was like to *have* money, but all those cups of coffee were making me thirsty, which was weird because I'd never tasted coffee. Suddenly, though, I was craving a huge cup with lots of cream and sugar, a chocolate chip muffin, and those little cubes of sugar that crunched against your teeth. I'd watched Jed eat one of those on every single birthday; they were his favorite. Now, I wanted one so badly I could feel saliva pooling in my mouth and my stomach grumbling loudly enough that I'm sure someone could hear it. But I had not a penny, so on I walked.

As I moved through the city, most people ignored me, which felt
normal, but from time to time, someone would catch my eye and
smile. At first, those smiles felt great, new as I was to being seen,
but in time, they just made me feel lonelier and more scared. I
had no way of contacting anyone, no money to buy food, and no
place to even sit down.

But then, I remembered what Shelby said about Jed knowing
how to find me. The very thought of her made my teeth ache,
but I sure hoped she was right.

Finally, I wandered up a hill and came upon the Black Dog
Salvage shop and laughed. Mrs. Wilson loved the show *Salvage
Dawgs* with the two men who did architectural salvage and
owned this shop. In fact, she loved it so much that Mr. Wilson
had gotten a bigger satellite TV package for her birthday *just* so
she could watch it all the time. Now, just the sight of the big
rocket in front of the store made me feel better. I walked inside,
made my way into the back of the big warehouse and sat down
on a sofa, trying to look like I might make a purchase.

No one paid me any mind, and I must have dozed off because
the next thing I knew, Jed was shaking my shoulder and saying
my name. "Mavis. Mavis, it's us. Wake up. Are you okay?"

I opened my eyes slowly, a bit embarrassed to find myself
slumped over against the arm of the sofa made from truck parts.
I smiled. "I'm fine, bud. Just fell asleep. It's been kind of a long
night."

Jed laughed. "I'll say." Then, he helped me up, and we made our
way to the front of the shop. One of the guys from the TV show
—Robert—was there, signing an autograph, and he winked at
me as he said, "We all need a good nap from time to time." The
color flashed up my cheeks again, but I also felt grateful. Kindness shows up in all sorts of ways.

When we came into the parking lot, Alonso and Shelby were

there, and I didn't hesitate. I got my hands around Shelby's throat faster than I had ever known I could move. "You traitor," I screamed as I shook her.

But Alonso wrapped his arms around my shoulders and pulled me back, bear-hugging me to his chest while I screamed. Shelby just smiled, and that made me even madder—until Jed stepped in front of me and said, "It was part of the plan, Mavis."

I was so mad I could hardly hear him.

"Mavis, please, breathe." Shelby had come closer again. "I made that call so you could hear me. I needed you to hear me. Do you understand?"

I didn't understand. Not at all. What good did it do to scare an old lady senseless with nonsense like that?

"I needed you to know that someone was coming for you, that Jed was coming for you. I needed you to keep hope."

I was totally confused. "So, wait, what? Are you some kind of double agent or something?"

"Not something. I am a double agent. For years, I've let Poke believe I was working for him because I feared for my kids. But really, I was spying on him for us." She was looking me square in the face, and I didn't really want to—anger feels good sometimes—but I believed her.

I started to calm down, and Alonso's arms loosened from around my body.

"What we didn't count on," Alonso said, "was that you'd escape. How did you escape?"

I looked around at all the cool junk in the parking lot and then at the crowd of shoppers trying to look like they weren't looking at us. "Can we go somewhere else, and then I'll tell you?"

"Sure," Alonso said and pointed me toward a white panel van like the ones kidnappers always use in those police shows. I really needed to watch less TV.

Once we were on the road back to the farm, I told them about how I figured out how to go invisible, and I was feeling pretty smug—until I looked at Jed, and he looked even more like he'd swallowed the canary. "What are you grinning at?"

"I've been wondering when you'd figure it out, Mavis."

I furrowed my brown eyes and looked at him through lowered eyebrows. "What do you mean?"

"I mean, you've been able to do it all along—well, at least since I first came to the village, but it just took *you* figuring that out for you to actually do it."

When had this kid gotten so dang smart?

"Same with me," he said. "I didn't know I could draw that way or see people's powers, and I definitely had no idea it was because I'm telepathic."

Ah, there it was. I knew that telepathy was a thing, and I wasn't sure I liked it. "So, you can read my mind?"

"No, not exactly. It's more like I can read around you, see sort of what you see, like the shapes of stuff. I'm not explaining this well." He looked at Shelby.

"Jed is what we call a visual telepath. You're thinking of a verbal telepath. Verbal telepaths read thoughts, the words we use to think. Emotional telepaths read, well, emotions. But visual telepaths like Jed see what other people see."

Suddenly, it made sense. Jed was seeing people the way they really are: their secrets, their shadows, their shames. I didn't know if that was entirely a good thing, but I sure was grateful for it now.

"You saw me at the salvage place?"

"Yep. Well, I saw everywhere you were, but the salvage place was the first place I recognized."

"The rocket."

"Exactly."

I'd never been more grateful for do-it-yourself television and Mrs. Wilson's never-ending love of old stuff.

We sat in silence for a few minutes as Alonso drove us out of the city back toward the farm. Shelby and Jed were on milk crates in the back, and they'd given me—out of courtesy for the old woman, I expect—the front seat. I didn't resist. My hips had had a hard night.

As we got off I-81, a flush of panic washed through me, and I started to sweat. I kept looking around, sure that Poke's people were waiting for us and I'd be caught again. But no one else looked worried, and that helped.

As we made the final turn toward the farm, Shelby said, "We took some precautions, Mavis. You're safe here. I'm sorry we didn't do them before. We didn't realize we'd been followed, but no one that we don't want to get in can get in now."

I wanted to be brave and trusting, but I was still reeling a bit from her traitor-to-double-agent moment. "You're sure?"

"Positive. Look."

From the farm lane, I could see the farmhouse and the barn below us, same as always, but I figured I needed to look harder to see whatever Shelby thought I should. So, I tried to go into the space I found when I went invisible, and there it was, big as day, a tightly-woven net around the farm. It stretched from all the way over to the edge of the Wilsons' property, to the road, and then back to the woods like a dome.

"It's like a spider web." I was awed.

"Exactly." Jed was speaking quietly. "I would have made it a dome, like a force field, but LaKeemba said that even innocent things, like birds and butterflies, bounce off of domes, and that can draw attention. But with a net, the animals and bugs can pass through, just like normal. It's just the big stuff that can't get through. We all helped to put it up."

"This is what we had back at the village?"

While Alonso parked by the barn, he said, "It is. Only then, it was smaller. It worked, but not like this one. This one is super-charged." He gave Jed a high five as Jed jumped from the back of the van.

I felt a bit better, but I figured I wasn't going to feel all better—maybe ever.

I didn't have time to wallow though. LaKeemba had called a meeting, and this time the Wilsons were invited.

JEDIDIAH

When Alonso had first suggested we tell my parents about my abilities, I wasn't sure about it. I'd been hiding what I could do—even the sort of lame version from before—for so long that it felt kind of weird to tell them now. A little part of me was excited though. I'd wanted to tell them so many times.

When he explained that sometimes people got more powerful when they had the support of the people they loved most, it was an easy decision.

I was still a little worried about one thing: Mavis. I figured I could tell my family that I could see things other people couldn't. But it was totally another thing to tell them that your imaginary friend wasn't imaginary and hadn't ever been imaginary. I didn't think they'd like that Mavis had heard all our private family stuff, especially "the talks" that I dreaded so much. The sex one, yeah, but also the ones about bullying and about homophobia and about racism. My parents were very big on being very open, but I wasn't sure they would like that they'd been that open with someone they couldn't even see.

Still, it felt weird doing all this stuff right there on the farm and having to lie to them about it, even if Sharon was the one doing the lying. So, I was glad to just get it all out there.

That morning, LaKeemba had suggested I tell them about all this before we left to find Mavis. She said it was important they understand what was happening, especially since they had met Mavis and knew she was missing.

"They'll want to help, don't you think?" she'd asked.

I knew they would.

They did, and I was so glad my parents knew the whole story, even though I could see how worried they were. The worry seemed more real though, more like them than before when they'd been convinced to think it wasn't a big deal.

We told them about Poke, about how he'd been trying to trap people in the village for years now, about how Charlie was his son, and about how Mavis was, actually, my imaginary friend. I saved that part for last because I figured it would be the weirdest.

"I kind of wondered when you introduced her," Dad said.

"You knew?"

"'Knew' may be too strong a word. 'Sensed' might be better."

"Yeah, Mavis was always kind of a weird. She didn't talk like a kid, and she always knew the shows we watched and understood them. The one time you watched NCIS with us, you asked a billion questions. But the next morning, you were suddenly talking about whether it was actually possible to get a DNA sample from a hair follicle. You were five."

I felt a little silly then, but my parents were looking at me with those stupid smiles they got when they were about to hug me.

As soon as I was wrapped up in their arms, I said against Mom's shoulder, "I told you she was real."

She laughed. "That you did, honey. That you did."

After that, they were all business. They didn't both have successful careers and keep this farm running by goofing off. "What do we need to do?"

LaKeemba didn't hesitate. "We need you to let people know they can't come to the farm for a bit. Maybe some story about an illness."

"Got it. I've got a staph infection from a bad cut on the barbed wire fence around the pasture. I need complete bed rest. Leon, you'll tell Christy?" My mom was on it.

"Christy's our mail carrier. Let her know, and everyone will know by the end of the day," he told LaKeemba. "She's supposed to bring some parts I ordered today. I'll catch her up on the farm gossip when she does." He gave me a wink.

"Great." LaKeemba stood up. "We need to get Mavis back first, but then, we need you all to come to a meeting. Jed, Alonso, and Shelby are waiting for you. I expect you have some sense of where to go?"

I stood up and said, "Yes, ma'am." Then, I looked at my parents before peering at LaKeemba. "You'll explain what I can do."

"I will. Be safe."

I waved and ran out the door.

I hadn't even seen Charlie sitting on the stairs.

18

*B*y the time I had gotten something to eat, taken a pee break (again), and gotten back to the fire pit by the barn, everyone was already there, including the Wilsons and Charlie. Everybody seemed totally at ease. I, however, wanted to duck back into the woods and pretend I was peeing again.

When I looked around for a seat, Mrs. Wilson pulled an empty camp chair out from beside her. "Sit with me, Mavis? It's so good to see you. I understand you've been around all this time, but I have missed you. I'm glad you're back—all the way back." Then, she stood up and gave me a back-cracking hug.

I tried to wipe the tears away quickly as I sat down.

LaKeemba began immediately. "Friends, we have a war on our hands. But not the kind of war where we go into battle. No, this is the kind of war that we fight with strategy, with our minds, and with our abilities. It's time for us to make a plan to rid ourselves of Poke's control once and for all."

Heads nodded all around the fire pit.

"But first, we need to talk about what happened to Mavis. In our community, we don't hide bad things, and we don't pretend they didn't happen. Mavis, if you're comfortable, would you tell us what happened to you?"

I felt a little shy, but something about the idea of not hiding bad things felt right, good, so I stood up and told them the story—about Glass, about hearing Shelby, about using my invisibility to sneak away. When people applauded at the part of the story when I opened the front door, I stood up a little straighter. I guess that *was* something to be proud of.

When I finished, I took my seat again, and Mrs. Wilson squeezed my hand. "Mavis, do you know why they took you?"

I didn't hesitate. "To capture y'all."

"Right." Shelby stood then. "That's been the plan all along. To capture all of us and take us back as slaves." A grumble passed through the crowd, but I could tell they weren't surprised, just angry. "Isn't that right, Charlie?"

My head spun to where Charlie sat with Jed on the ground by the fire. His face was bright red, redder than his hair, and he looked like he was angry. At first, I thought he was mad because of what his father planned to do—that's why I was mad, after all —but then, a sly grin crossed his face.

"And they'll get you, too. You nig—"

"That's enough, son." Mr. Wilson stood up. "We don't use that word in this place or in any place under any circumstance."

Charlie stood up then. "But these ni—these people. They are meant to work for us. You let them be here without paying, without even helping. That's not how it's supposed to be."

I saw Mr. Wilson's face soften then. "Son, these people. . . These people are our friends. They are our equals. They don't belong to us. They don't work for us. They don't owe us anything. They are our friends." He walked closer to Charlie. "I know you've been taught a lot of things—maybe not so much with words, but by what you've seen. You've been taught to think of black people as owing you something, like you're doing them a favor by giving them work and a place to sleep and food to eat. But those things, Charlie, those things are simply the basic necessities of life. Giving them to someone doesn't mean you've done them a favor. It simply means you've been a decent person."

"But Papa says ni—I mean, black people—need us to take care of them, that they can't survive out there."

"Helen, do you have your phone?" He took it from Mrs. Wilson and then gestured for Charlie to sit down.

Charlie sat beside him on the grass.

"See this man, Charlie?" He held the phone over to Charlie. "This is Daniel Hale Williams. He's the first man to ever do a heart transplant. I bet you can't even imagine that you could take one person's heart and put it into another person's body, but in a few decades, that will be possible."

I couldn't tell if Charlie was more stunned by the phone or by the information, but he did seem to be listening.

"This woman. . . This is Oprah Winfrey. The businesses, houses, and other things that she owns are worth $2.4 billion. That's a two with seven zeroes behind it. She's one of the wealthiest people in America."

"That woman? That ni—" He looked at Dad. "What word am I supposed to use?"

"African American, Charlie. We call people in America with African ancestry African American when we are speaking of them formally."

Charlie nodded, but he didn't look totally convinced.

Mr. Wilson did another search. "This man. . . He is my favorite painter. His name is Jean-Michel Basquiat. See this painting of his? He brings in symbols and uses images that refer back to Africa but are also very American."

I noticed that Mr. Wilson did not mention that Basquiat was bisexual, something he'd shared openly with Jed when they'd talked about the painter, but maybe he figured that was too much for Charlie for today. He was probably right.

"Does this look like people who can't take care of themselves, Charlie? People who need white people to help them survive?"

Charlie looked fully and truly confused, but he shook his head.

"That's right. I know that most of the white people from when you come from believe that, but it's just not true. That's a lie a lot of people have told and believed for a long time because it makes things easier for them. Slavery makes your life easier, doesn't it, Charlie? You don't have to wash your own clothes or weed your own garden or take care of your own animals, right?"

Charlie looked like he wanted to disagree, but after a pause, he mumbled, "Right."

"And your parents don't have to do any of those things, right?"

Charlie's voice was very, very soft, but we still heard him. "Don't have a mama."

Mrs. Wilson got up then and scooched Jed over so she could sit beside Charlie, too. "Oh, Charlie. That's hard." Charlie leaned against her a bit.

Mr. Wilson put a hand on Charlie's arm. "Think about all the things you and your dad get to do because all the people you force to work for you do the things you need to survive. Looks like maybe the lies you and your dad have been told are actually backwards, don't they? Seems like the people you enslave take care of you, doesn't it?"

Charlie gave a sort of half nod.

"We can talk about this more, Charlie." Mr. Wilson stood up. "But I don't want to hear you using that word again, you understand?"

Another mumble. "Yes, sir."

It was only then that I realized that everyone else had stayed silent. They were paying attention to the conversation—I could tell by the way their ears tilted toward the Charlie and Mr. Wilson—but they were also trying to stay apart from it.

I'd have to figure that out later because LaKeemba had stood up again. "Charlie here has been spying on us. He has reported our location to Poke, and he is the reason they were able to kidnap Mavis."

I looked over at the boy, the one who had turned me in, and I was ready to be spitting mad. But when I saw his face, how close to crying he was, I just felt bad for him.

"We know, Charlie, but we also know that it felt like the right thing to you, like you were helping everybody, isn't that right?" LaKeemba's voice was gentle, and she was looking at Charlie with more compassion than I was able to muster in the moment.

Charlie's head moved up and down almost imperceptibly.

"And I expect there was some fear that made you do it, too, wasn't there?"

Now, the tears wouldn't stop, and Charlie dropped his head into his legs, his shoulders bouncing.

"You didn't deserve to be treated that way, Charlie. You hear me?" LaKeemba had walked over and crouched down so her mouth was right by Charlie's ear. "You are important and beloved, just like the rest of us. And no one should ever lay a hand on you." Her voice was quiet, but it carried.

She stood then. "Poke is a man of his time, and while he is responsible for his actions, horrible, terrible, cruel actions," she glanced over at Charlie again, "he also is simply doing what the people around him taught him to do."

"Hurt people hurt people." Jed's voice was soft but sure. "That's what Ms. Cecil, the guidance counselor, always says."

LaKeemba strode back over to the fire, and she seemed taller just now. "That's right, Jed, and while it's not good for the people who get hurt, it's also not good for the people who do the hurting. It twists them, makes them uglier versions of themselves. So today, we're making a plan to stop Poke, but also to help him."

I wasn't sure I loved that idea. It felt too woo-woo, too easy to me. I wanted Poke to be punished. I wanted him to be enslaved, to be the one who had to do back-breaking work all day for no pay.

But I also knew that LaKeemba was right. The only way to make things better was to break the cycle.

"What do we do?" My voice rang out across the hayfield, and I shrank back with embarrassment into the blanket Shelby had wrapped around my shoulders when I'd sat down.

"Good question." LaKeemba began to walk around the circle. "All of you who have abilities that let you manipulate the elements, move over there by Charlie. Those of you who can change the way people think or feel or appear, over by Sharon." She pointed across the circle from me. "Those of you who see the future, the past, or the secrets, with me."

I watched Jed move toward LaKeemba, and I realized that's exactly what he was—the boy who could see secrets.

I was still sitting there when Sharon waved her arms over her head to get my attention. "Get over here, Mavis. You're with us."

I squinted at her a bit. I was with them. Why? I couldn't do any —then I smiled and made my way over to my group.

$\mathcal{T}$he plan was elaborate but so natural that it felt like it was going to be easy. Fortunately, none of us were dumb enough to think it actually would be. But we couldn't waste any time, so we set to work.

The first step was another bait and switch, and Jed went into action again. This time with help from Alonso and an older woman named Bernice, who could make people see what she wanted them to see. Their role was to show up in as many places and times as possible and leave Easter eggs—I learned that term from Jed and his plethora of video games—for Poke's people to find. We wanted them to think we were splitting up, trying to hide more easily by separating.

The trio traveled around. Jed would find Poke's man or woman and get Alonso and Bernice into position. Then, Alonso would touch the Poke's lackey as he or she passed by, giving them a little dose of power to make Bernice's vision both more vivid and longer lasting. Then, Bernice would project an image of one or two of the villagers there in that place and time. She'd make sure their faces were visible so that Poke's flunkies would be absolutely sure. Finally, Jed would take a look to be sure they hadn't been spotted, and then they'd head out.

Their work combined with a bit of illusion work by a teenager named Tequon led anyone who was watching the Wilson place to believe that we were all in the process of packing up and leaving the Wilsons' farm, a few people at a time.

From all reports delivered by the prophecy and prediction team, as I took to calling LaKeemba's group, it was working. Their visions were getting more and more positive, and Jed told us at night around the fire, that Poke's people seemed more and more confused each day.

At the same time, the people pushers—Charlie and his group, led by a thin reed of a man named Montrose—were building an arsenal of tools that would disable but not injure and a strategy for how to use those weapons to capture Poke and his henchmen (and henchwomen—if that's a word).

Our group's job—I thought of us as the Mighty Morphing Minions (I loved those one-eyed, yellow, capsule-shaped creatures)—was to prepare to infiltrate Poke's plantation, destroy any records related to slavery, and then lead Poke into our trap. The woman who could put people to sleep—I finally learned that her name was Ethel—was on our team as was Lizzie, the shadow-turner. Then, there was Sharon, the sweet talker. I kept imagining what our superhero outfits would look like—no tights, that was for sure. My thighs didn't do well in tights.

By the end of the third day, we'd taken all our preliminary steps and set all the traps, and now, we simply had to put the plan into action. I could barely sleep.

The next morning, when I woke up—sleep never eludes me long —I donned my Poke-visiting dress again. This time, I got Lizzie to tie the lacings, wise enough to not let Shelby truss me up again. I liked breathing too much for that.

Then, we gathered by the fire for one last village meeting. Jed's trio had already been out that morning to plant one more sighting, this time of him and me in Charlottesville. We figured Poke was smart enough to know Jed wouldn't go too far from home, but we knew it would be useful to have us seen out and about, just to dispel any doubt that we weren't with any of the villagers. Apparently, Jed told me later, we were spotted toilet papering the Robert E. Lee statue downtown. I liked that idea.

I expect what LaKeemba said was like one of those rousing speeches that come just before the climax of every sports movie, but I could hardly pay attention. I just kept imagining what would happen if we failed. Images of my friends being whipped or put in the stocks for days in the hot sun came to mind. And that possibility was horrible, but then I imagined them being sold away from each other—Shelby's kids sold, Mercy sold to a different place than LaKeemba—and I shivered. Slavery was bad enough when you had to do it with your family. To do it without them seemed impossible.

This had to work. It just had to.

Then, everyone began to move, and I found myself on the way to Poke's plantation, this time in the back of a wagon with Ethel, Sharon, a woman I'd just met named Shelva, and a couple of the men, Elwood and Dean. I'd seen Elwood rip a tree out of the ground back at the farm when he heard it was dead and Mr. Wilson needed to cut it down. It was impressive. Dean had a power a lot like Sharon's, except when he spoke to someone with intention, he could take over their bodies for a few minutes. I was glad for their powers, but also for their presence. I'd gone to Poke's place alone once, and I didn't want to go again.

Marcus was driving the wagon, and it was only as we loaded that I realized he was there for a specific reason: he could talk to animals. I kept trying to keep Eddie Murphy as Dr. Doolittle out of my mind—Marcus was thin and very short, so the physical resemblance wasn't there—but I couldn't. I watched to see if a guinea pig would crawl out of his pocket.

Our plan was very simple. Just before we reached Poke's lane, everyone would get off the wagon except for Marcus and me. We were going to pretend like we were dumb enough to try and fool Poke with some story about wanting to have his help settling me into a role here in this time, that I just didn't feel right going back now that I wasn't imaginary anymore. We knew Poke wouldn't buy it, but we thought maybe we could distract him long enough. It had worked once; maybe it would work again?

Meanwhile, the rest of the crew would sneak in and hide near the big house. Dean was prepared to stop any of the white folks, or strangely loyal slaves, and redirect them away. Elwood would stick close to me as a bodyguard of sorts. For a brief moment when I'd first heard this, I imagined myself as a slightly older Taylor Swift with her entourage of strong men. I liked it.

Sharon was going to get near Poke and talk him into forgetting everything about all of us, and Shelby was there as a last resort. If all else failed, she'd burn the whole place to the ground as soon as Dean talked everyone he could into leaving. We didn't want anyone to get hurt, but we also knew that drastic action might be necessary to keep more people from being hurt in the long run.

As the wagon approached the Poke place, I had a sudden flash of panic, and it must have shown because Sharon reached across and put her hand on my arm. "You okay?"

"Oh, yes, yes. But Charlie? What about Charlie? If we have to set a fire. . ."

Sharon let out a hard sigh. "No one told you." Her jaw was set in a firm line. "Charlie ran away last night. I expect we're about to see him."

"He what? He came back here? After all he's seen, with what he can do. . . Why would he do that? Jed told him he probably wouldn't be able to come back. Why would he do that?"

But I knew my answer. People return to what they know a whole lot easier than they take to something new, even if what they know is the worst thing for them. Still, I wanted to cry.

I didn't have much time to dwell on Charlie though because we were close. The others jumped off and dashed into the woods as we approached the plantation, and I sat up a little straighter as Marcus turned down the farm lane.

Again, I was awed by how beautiful the place was—the columns of trees on each side of the lane, the beautiful mansion with its wide front porch just ahead, the carefully tended pastures and fences. In our time, this beauty was what took all those people on those tours of places like Montpelier and Monticello.

But, as we got closer, I saw the slaves again, backs bent, weariness a feature of their bones. In our time, people don't usually think of this part of slavery, or they don't want to. I know the big plantations have tours and exhibits about slavery, but I imagined a lot of the guests didn't even look at those exhibits and probably resented being forced to remember what had created all this beauty.

As we pulled up to the house, Poke and Charlie came out onto the porch. Poke's arm was draped around his son's shoulders, but one look at Charlie told me that this wasn't a tender father-son moment. The boy looked scared to death.

"Well, well, Mavis, what brings you here? Your time in a locked room didn't deter you from staying involved with this lot." He gestured toward Marcus, who sort of snarled.

"Actually," I tried to step down from the wagon as gracefully as I could, "that's why I'm here. I'm hoping to get your help." I whisked my eyes toward Marcus as if indicating I didn't want him to hear.

Poke either bought my line or felt like playing along with the ruse and said, "Get that wagon to the back of the house, boy."

I winced at his dismissive tone.

Marcus clicked and sent the horses on around. As they turned toward the back, I saw him lean over the horses, and one of them flicked an ear in his direction.

"Mavis, I'm not quite sure what to say, but I'm a reasonable man. Why don't you come up here and have some tea? Charlie, get Bettey to bring us a pitcher. We may be here a while."

Charlie looked half panicked, but he did as he was told, looking back over his shoulder at me as he went.

I climbed the steps to the house and took a seat in the same chair I'd occupied a few days before. The view was the same—people working and watching while trying to look like they weren't.

After Bettey placed the pitcher and two glasses on the table between Poke and me, he took a long sip and then said, "So, what's your proposition, Mavis?"

I sputtered on my own swallow. "Proposition? I don't know what you mean."

"You're here to offer a trade, I expect. The children for something of yours in return."

"Well, now that you mention it. . ." I felt like maybe I should go with this line of thought for a minute. It might buy us the time we needed. "We were wondering what you would take to let the children go free."

Poke stood and started pacing around the edge of the porch. Again, I couldn't tell if he was really thinking or if he was playing me for a fool, and I didn't love that he was looking out at his slaves. He might spot someone. I took a deep breath. There was nothing I could do but play my part. I had to just let him do his thing.

"Give me Shelby and Alonso. Oh, and that girl, Lizzie. I like her." He turned to face me then, and the sneer on his face made my skin crawl. "Give me those three, and I'll let all the children go. I'll even give you the rest of their papers that you didn't manage to steal from me last time."

There it was. "No deal. We don't barter in people, Mr. Poke." As soon as I spoke, I realized I'd blown my cover altogether. "We" is not the term people use when they want to part ways with someone.

Poke's face broke into a huge grin. "Well, if it's not for a barter, what brings you here, Mavis?"

I stared into the farmyard, trying to think of something to say and smiled. "Oh, no. . . Fire!" Sure enough, a thin stream of smoke was coming out of the stables across the farmyard.

Fire always gets people moving, and Poke was no exception. He started shouting. "Get the wagons. Bring the barrels. Grab the buckets. Fire! Fire! Fire!"

I almost felt bad for him, but I didn't have time for that nonsense. I had work to do.

JEDIDIAH

I know Mavis wanted me to stay back at the farm, but that was less likely to happen than a tick to not bite a dog's rear. As soon as the wagon rolled out from the village, I high-tailed my rear over to Poke's place. I got there just in time to see Shelby light the fire and hear Poke yelling.

Around the back of the house, I found Marcus and his wagon along with Poke's two wagons and all eight of his horses. They were ready to carry everyone back to the oak and then on back to the farm. One of the wagons was already full of the children, and Marcus sent the horses on around the side of the house away from the barn so that they could get out while Poke and his overseer were busy at the fire. The other slaves were streaming out from the fields and cabins, too, and soon, both the other wagons and most of the horses were on their way through the woods back to Heavenland.

As they were leaving, Marcus caught a glimpse of me and shouted, "Ride with Mavis. That girl there," he pointed at a beautiful chocolate-brown horse, "she says she'll carry you both. Don't dawdle. You know what happens at four."

I did know, and I had no plans to hang around any longer than it would take to get Mavis out. I went up the back steps of the house and slipped inside, expecting to see Mavis in the front parlor where she'd said Poke's desk was. But she wasn't there.

Just then, I heard a big crash. When I ran out onto the porch, I saw one of the pole barns slump over. I caught a glimpse of Elwood ducking around the building. Then, I heard a shout and spun around to see Dean being held tight by one of Poke's men. He was gripped around the chest, but he seemed calm. I saw his lips move, and just like that, the man dropped his hold and turned to walk up the farm lane. Dean saw me and threw up a wave before heading off. I wouldn't want to get a scolding from Dean, that's for sure.

I was just about to head back inside to look for Mavis when a firm hand grabbed my arm. I yanked it away and turned to see Charlie there. I'd heard he'd run away, and I had no time for someone who would support the kind of hatefulness his dad did. But I saw tears on Charlie's cheeks, and as much as I wanted to just turn away, I couldn't.

"You told him." I could see it all over him—the darkness, the embarrassment, the bruises.

Charlie nodded. "He told me that no one like that could be a part of his family, so I'd best find somewhere to go." He let out a long groan. "But I got nowhere to go, Jed."

I'd seen Poke's twisted pain when he'd come to the village—the lingering memory of a mother who'd burned him with a hot poker when he broke a cup. 'Hurt people hurt people.' Mrs. Cecil was right.

I sighed. "Yes, you do. Come on."

"They won't take me back, Jed. I betrayed them."

"I know. You told them how to get to Mavis. We all know. But the thing is, we all do bad stuff. We all mess up." I thought of Dad and the way he reminded me that mistakes were just lessons on the way to success. "It may take a bit, but it'll be okay. I think most people get it."

I didn't quite get it, but I figured if I thought about it a bit, maybe heard a little more about what it was like to live with Poke, I might get it more. Didn't have time to do that now, though. "We've gotta go. Help me find Mavis."

We sprinted inside and back into the front parlor. There, in mid-air, was a big stack of papers. "Mavis!" *I ran over and hugged the space behind the pile.*

"Got 'em all," *she said.*

"Then, let's go," *I shouted, and we headed out the back door. Mavis and I jumped on the brown horse, and Charlie swung himself up onto the back of a gray mare.*

"What time is it, Jed?" *Mavis said as I saw her hands appear around my waist, where she was holding on tight.*

"Three thirty! We've got to ride."

We were hauling tail up the farm lane, Mavis and I in the lead with Charlie right behind us, when we heard Poke shouting as his horse gained on us. I started to panic. He couldn't follow us, not this soon.

"Charlie, do something," *I shouted over my shoulder.*

I couldn't see what Charlie was doing, but all of a sudden, the sound of horse hooves softened a bit. I looked back to see Poke and his horse in mid-stride, stuck in time.

20

*J*t's amazing what you don't know when you think you know everything about a person. I mean, Jed had never ridden a horse before. I knew that, but I'd never thought about it. I needn't have worried though. That boy knew what he was doing—or maybe the horse did. That was probably more likely.

We rode down the lane, and I was already terrified, but when that mare turned into the woods and didn't slow down, I thought I might break Jed's ribs I was grabbing him so hard. That horse weaved and dodged through those trees like she was racing the Preakness, and in fifteen minutes, we were at the oak.

I would have liked to just keep riding right into our time, but we needed to be sure we crossed the right way. So at the tree, all three of us dismounted and sent the horses on around, sure that Marcus had given them careful instructions. We had not even considered leaving them behind to live with Poke. In fact, given the roaming chickens and squealing pigs I'd seen on our way off the plantation, I expected that Marcus had freed all the animals and given them explicit instructions about how to survive or find new caretakers.

Now, though, we had to prepare because we had less than ten minutes to get back to the farm, and we needed to be sure we made this crossing perfectly. No time for flub-ups. No chance for do-overs.

"Charlie, you know what to do, right? You have to think about our farm." Jed was directing Charlie with careful attention. "You can think about all this stuff later. Now, though, you have to focus. We don't have much time."

Charlie was as white as a sheet, and I could see the beginnings of some pretty big shakes coming on. "Jed, you take him. I'll be right behind you."

Jed gave me a puzzled stare but then nodded. He wrapped an arm around Charlie's waist. "We're almost home, Charlie. You're going to be the brother I always wanted. Think of the farm, Charlie. You ready?"

Charlie gave the tiniest of nods, and then they were gone.

I took a few last looks at the forest and rested my hand on the bark of this beautiful pin oak. As I walked around her—she was definitely a her—I said, "Thank you, old friend. You have served us well." She trembled beneath my touch again, and then, I let go.

Everyone was gathered by the tree when I reached the other side. A lot of parents and children were huddled up together, reunited. I scanned the crowd, saw Charlie with a blanket around his shoulders and Mrs. Wilson by his side, and then I saw Jed and his dad standing near Alonso with the chainsaw.

A gentle quiet fell over the group as we prepared to say good-bye. Then, just at the edge of my hearing, I heard a song begin. Not quite words but almost like I was hearing a lullaby from the other room. It was coming from the trees in the forest, a funeral lament. It was beautiful and made me think of golden light and the first green of spring. There was hope in it, hope growing alongside the sadness.

We let the song carry for a few moments, but when we dared wait no longer, Alonso started the chainsaw. LaKeemba came forward and poured a thin stream of water at the tree's roots. She rested her forehead against the bark for a minute, and when she turned back, tears tunneled down her cheeks.

Alonso stepped forward and began the cut.

I want to tell you that it didn't hurt the tree, that she didn't feel it. But that would, of course, be a lie. Because even when a death is good and noble, even when it's better than a whole host of other things far more terrible, it still hurts. When our tree fell, we wept for her. She gave herself to us, and she died willingly, which is a great gift to give even when you have no choice.

As I walked back to my tent, I thought about all the awfulness in the world that brings about death, about how sometimes good people have to die to stop the harm that other people do in the world. It's not fair. It's never fair. But there is a beauty that arises from those deaths. A gift that comes out of the loss.

THE DAYS after the tree's felling were quiet ones. We made plans —normal plans about jobs and school and such—and we sat around telling the stories of travel and time. Mostly, I listened because the stories I knew weren't really mine—not the ones from before.

Now, though, now I had stories, and I'd have lots more to come. I had no doubt.

In time, the Wilsons convinced everyone to stay, and folks built a little gathering of houses in the back pasture, not quite as close as in Heavenland but close enough to be neighbors still. This time, it looked more like a commune. The county tried to come and claim it was an illegal development, but since most of the houses were yurts and, thus, not permanent, they didn't have much recourse.

Soon, Mercy, Cato, and Lizzie were riding the bus to school with Jed, and Charlie was catching the later bus to the high school. He was getting along fine. Sharon got him into the foster care system and got the Wilsons assigned as his foster parents, and we all knew it wouldn't take long for them to adopt him.

Jed was back to riding his bike up and down the lane at breakneck speed. It was a glorious sight to see. Now, though, I sat on the porch of my own yurt and watched him pedal, standing up as he put his arms wide above his head. I slept in my own bed and had my own shower, and most nights, I had company over for dinner. It was glorious.

ONE EVENING, a few months after we felled the pin oak, Cato came flying back onto the farm. I don't know how it happened to be that he came upon me first, but he did. "Mavis, Mavis, come see." He grabbed me up out of my Adirondack chair on the porch and dragged me into the woods. We went a different way —back more toward the Lacy's place than the village had been before—and skirted the edge of the woods. And there, bright in her beautiful white bark standing next to a tiny stream, was a giant sycamore.

I couldn't tell you if she'd been there all along. Maybe. Maybe not. But she was here now, and she was waiting.

I smiled down at Cato. "Where and when do you want to go?"

He took my hand, and I bent down to hear his whisper. Then, we were off.

JEDIDIAH

That day, when the tree fell, I heard the cries of the forest. It was awful. But even worse was the way that evil, that thing that pushed Poke further toward hate, got stronger because of the sorrow. It was as if it fed on it.

What it didn't know was that I fed on the sorrow, too. It gave me purpose and stamina. It gave me focus.

I was starting to see that evil's shape, and I knew that once we could see that evil for what it was, we'd have a chance. It couldn't stay a secret forever.

THE MAP THAT CAN TWIST TIME

Chapter 1

*T*he air was as hot and thick as cat's fur, but in the lake, Jed and Charlie didn't much care. I, however, was fanning myself with a 2006 copy of *Better Homes and Gardens* that I had found on the coffee table in the cabin the Wilsons had rented for the week. I am not a fan of summer. Nope, not a bit. Give me a January day anytime. I can always put on more clothes, but for the sake of decency, there's only so much a person can take off.

Still, the evening was nice. The day was turning over to the purple of night, and as the boys climbed out of the lake, I watched the fireflies begin to flicker in the tree line. Behind me, I could hear the faint voices of Mr. and Mrs. Wilson as they had their one beer each and grilled hamburgers up on the deck at the cabin. *This is about perfect,* I thought.

Then, I immediately regretted letting my thoughts go that far to good. All my 63, almost 64 years, have taught me that the world worked – Lord or no – in mysterious ways. You never knew what might jinx a perfectly good night such as this.

I was happy though; I was. It had been a few months since Jed and I'd had our adventure with the HeavenLand folks and since Charlie had come to live with the Wilsons after his own daddy had cut him off. The days had been good ones, even if it had taken a bit of getting used to having everybody seeing me and all. I'd been imaginary for a lot of years, and if I was honest, I sometimes missed the days when it was just Jed and me. Or maybe, I just kind of missed having Jed all to myself in a way.

But I did like how when I talked with folks they looked me in the eye, and I really liked to choose my seat at the movies and not have to move if someone accidentally sat down on me. It can be pretty awkward to have someone plot down in your lap. A little too personal, if you know what I mean.

I wasn't thinking about all that though by the lake that night. Nope, I was just relaxing in one of those Adirondack chairs that purport great comfort but are really just torture to get out of. The boys ran around and scooped fireflies out of the air. It was quiet, comfortable, easy. . . and so the sound of the bells came through the air crisp and clear.

If it had been winter, I would have thought Santa had come . . . or maybe that White Witch woman from Narnia. (That was Jed's favorite book when he was a kid, but that woman scared the bejeezus out of me.) But in summer, my first thought was *ice cream truck*, and that almost made the awkward climb out of my chair worth it.

Jed, Charlie, and I turned our faces toward the road, and Jed said, "What is that?"

Charlie said, "Wagon."

I looked at Jed, and then he looked at Charlie. "Wagon?"

"Yeah, those are horse bells. Lots of wagons use them. Help keep the wagon trains together at night, especially if it gets foggy." Charlie would know, being as how he'd grown up in the age of wagons and all.

Then, as if on cue, the fog rolled in across the lake, and I knew it. I'd jinxed the night. Me and my ridiculous optimism.

Around the bend in the road and from behind the house next door, a wagon rode up out of the fog. But not just any wagon. This one looked like the old-timey version of a camper, all wood and painted on the sides. A man sat hunched over the reins on the front bench, and even from where I stood, I could tell he was exhausted. I worried he might fall asleep right then and there.

But instead, he pulled up a little on the reins, and his two, small horses stopped. He gave them each a good scratch on the rump and then climbed down to the ground. Only then did he look up and say, "I've been looking for you three all over time. Shelby said I'd find you here."

Jed gave me a quick look and then jogged over to help the man lift a huge trunk out of the back of the wagon. That boy would carry the painting if a thief needed help stealing the Mona Lisa. Sometimes, his helpfulness really irked me. We did *not* need whatever was in that trunk, I could tell you that.

"Shelby sent you to us?" Charlie had taken the other end of the trunk, and they were headed toward the cabin after the man had pointed that direction.

"Wait, boys." I had finally begun to understand that my age gave me a sort of authority with most folks and that it also made people think I was responsible for these kids. The man looked up at me expectantly, but the boy kept on toward the cabin. Okay, other people thought I had authority; Jed and Charlie had no such delusions. "Jed, Charlie. Set that trunk down." This time the shrill edge to my voice got to them, I guess, because they dropped the trunk with a thud.

"Sir, forgive me for asking, but I expect you can understand we might be a bit leery of somebody just rolling up and asking us to carry a heavy object into our house."

The man looked at me out of the corner of his eye, and then I saw him wink at Jed. "You think I'm delivering a bomb, missy." He turned to me with a grin then.

I sputtered a bit. "Well, no sir. I am a bit surprised you know what a bomb is though." His wagon had made me imagine him being from some time before cars, and I'm pretty sure that bombs didn't predate cars. Maybe. I never was very good with history.

"Don't let my wheels fool you, Mavis. You know better than to think that just because a person looks one kind of way that they are that way."

I felt myself blush. He was right about that. Our travels through time and around the world had taught me that through and through, and yet, here I was forgetting everything I'd learned.

I blamed the fireflies. They had distracted me.

Charlie, never one to bother too much with manners, did me the favor of asking what I wanted to know though. "What's in the trunk, mister?"

"Name's Hercules, son. And we'll need to open that inside to answer that question."

I looked carefully at Hercules. He was small, wiry, almost, and now that he wasn't on that wagon, he didn't look quite so tired.

His head was slick in the middle, his brown skin shiny and surrounded by a thin ring of steel gray hair. If I didn't know better, I'd think he was quite old, but as Hercules himself had just reminded me, I did know better.

I gave Jed a little nod, and he and Charlie carried the trunk up onto the deck, where Mr. and Mrs. Wilson waited. I hung back to get a closer look at that wagon, but I still heard them introduce themselves and invite Hercules for burgers. You couldn't blame Jed for being helpful. His parents would invite the art thief over to dinner after Jed helped him carry out his spoils.

I made my way over to the horses, giving them a little scratch behind the ears as I circled around to read the wagon's side. "Hercules Pettit – Peddler of All the Things You Never Knew You Needed."

Peddler. I'd heard of them, but I imagined they drove wagons that rattled along with pots and pans and a random accordion hanging off the side, not this tidy, pretty thing. I was intrigued though . . . all the things I never knew I needed. I imagined there was a whole world full of them, and I wasn't sure I liked the idea that someone could bring them to me. Wasn't sure I liked that at all.

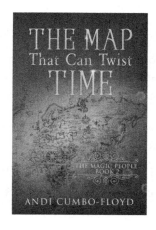

Order your copy here -

https://books2read.com/mapthatcantwisttime

GHOSTS. SPELLS. PEOPLE WITH WILD ABILITIES

If these are your faves, then come on over and get all the magical realism books your TBR can handle. Weekly emails of magical realism and fantasy, especially for young adults and the young at heart. Plus, a few notices about my own books, too.

Join my newsletter here:
andilit.com/magical-realism

ABOUT THE AUTHOR

Andi Cumbo-Floyd is a writer, editor, and historian who lives in the Blue Ridge Mountains with her husband, son, four dogs, and three cats. She writes regularly at andilit.com.

ALSO BY ANDI CUMBO-FLOYD

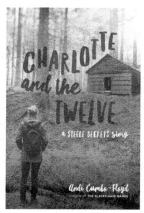

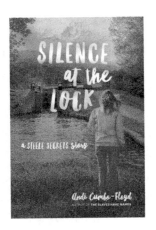

SILENCE
at the
LOCK

a STEELE SECRETS story

Andi Cumbo-Floyd
AUTHOR OF THE SLAVES HAVE NAMES

THE MAP
That Can Twist
TIME

THE MAGIC PEOPLE
BOOK 2

ANDI CUMBO-FLOYD

Made in the USA
Middletown, DE
13 May 2022

65585627R00096